THE EXODUS SERIES
SCORPION
AVINA ST. GRAVES

Scorpion by Avina St. Graves

Published by Avina St. Graves

Contact the author at author@avinastgraves.com

Character art by giulia_fw.arts

Editing by the Blue Couch Edits and Nessa's Lair

Cover by designsbycharly

ISBN Print 978-0-473-71830-5

ISBN eBook 978-0-473-71832-9

PLAYLIST

"Riptide" – *Vance Joy*
"Always Forever" – *Cults*
"Death by Rock and Roll" – *The Pretty Reckless*
"Snap Out Of It" – *Arctic Monkeys*
"Strange" – *Celeste*
"Breezeblocks" – *alt-J*
"I Can't Quit You Baby" – *Led Zeppelin*
"Small Death and the Codeine Scene" – Hozier
"When the Hurt Is Over" – *Mighty Sam McClain*
"The Night We Met" – *Lord Huron*
"New Person, Same Old Mistakes" – *Tame Impala*
"R U Mine" – *Arctic Monkeys*
"dance of the trees" – *Mikayla Geier*
"Abbey" – *Mitski*
"Heal" – *Tom Odell*
"Where's My Love – Acoustic" – *SYML*
"One More Hour" – *Tame Impala*
"Exit Music (For A Film)" – *Radiohead*
"But You" – *Alexandra Savior*

AUTHOR'S NOTE

I failed physics in high school, scraped a pass in math, and did phenomenally in research. This book is a product of that *hit it.*

The sniper-related information in this book was taken from military propaganda, inconsistent government information, *Mission Impossible*, a guy I know, and a bunch of dudes on Reddit who are playing devil's advocate.

Feel free to cite the facts from this book at parties. The only people who will be able to prove you wrong would be breaching national security.

Or they simply spend too long on the dark web.

In other important news, this novel sits within an interconnected series centralizing around what you'll soon learn as the *Reckoning*. This means that you may see characters and scenes within this book that appear in other novellas throughout this series.

If you want to read a book with complex characters, intense world-building, and a heavy plotline, this book is not for you. To put this novella-not-a-novella into context, it's roughly half the size of one of my full-length novels. *Scorpion* is too long to be considered a novella, but it's also *just* scrapping into the novel territory.

For pronunciation, Mathijs is Dutch, so his name is pronounced like "Ma-tays," like *Mathias* but with an "ae" sound at the end. Zalak is an Indian name, and her name is pronounced like "Zuh-luck."

PS. If you are not the person whom I share a house, a bed, and several animals with, you don't need to read this:

To my partner, I almost killed off the character I made of you. I am pleased to inform you that you have survived another book.

Do not mistake this as an invitation to try me. I *will* edit this book to change that. You'll do well not to question my levels of spite.

TRIGGERS

S ex, questionable use of a gun (yes, there's a pewpew scene), knife play (nonpenetrative), very bad gun safety practices, alcohol use, death of friends and family and many other people, trauma, PTSD, profanity, mental health issues, attempted suicide (on-screen), self-harm, use of sharp objects, parental abuse, financial abuse and manipulation, graphic violence, childhood trauma, blood, gore, and murder.

To the girls who see guns as potential sex toys, why stop there? It's time to get laid while using a rifle.

PROLOGUE

E very time I start to feel happy, I get a call from my mother. I haven't heard from her yet, but I know it's coming. My freedom never feels truly free because she's embedded herself in my brain like a tumor.

Mathijs's voice crackles through the headset as he belts out the song from our favorite band while drumming the cyclic control. In all his enthusiasm, he still keeps steady on the foot pedals, but it still feels like we might fall out of the sky at any second.

Death by helicopter isn't exactly on my wishlist.

Clutching my phone, I glance at the cockpit to double check nothing has gone out of whack since he started his performance. His dad would have an absolute field day if he knew Mathijs acted like this every time we flew—I suppose that's why his dad taught me how to fly as well.

Below, the mansions that seem so gigantic in person are

nothing more than lumps on the Earth, small and insignificant. Up ahead is the house and the empty space of asphalt out front that Mathijs thought would make a good helipad.

I almost had a damn heart attack when he flew in this morning to visit their family's vineyard in Paonia. Most boyfriends pick up their girls in a car or a motorcycle. Hell, I remember the days when he'd wait for me to sneak out while my parents weren't home, then I'd sit on the handlebars of his bike and roll my eyes every time he rang that annoying bell.

No, Mathijs Halenbeek is above all that now. He picks up his girlfriend in a $250K helicopter.

His hand lands on my lap, and I slap it away. "Focus," I snap.

Chuckling, he palms my thigh despite my protests. "Stop worrying." He pairs his words with a self-assured smile. "Your parents aren't meant to be back from Mumbai for another three days. Besides, it's the weekend, and all the staff who are likely to snitch aren't working. Your mom will never find out."

"I know that. But what I don't know is how far her crazy is willing to go. I wouldn't be surprised if she's installed hidden cameras around the house. For all I know, there could be a freaking recording device in my room to hear if Gaya and I are talking shit about her." My sister and I have gotten so paranoid about it that the only time we dare talk about our family is at school—even then we aren't confident that Mom hasn't planted some kind of bug on us.

Plus, it's becoming increasingly clear that our brother is a goddamn snitch. Gaya has youngest daughter syndrome and is clearly Papa's favorite, while Mom has undiagnosed BPD and embodies *Boy Mom*. That leaves me cursed with the dreaded *middle child disorder*.

"If she finds out that I'm with you, she's going to kill me—that's not an understatement." I run my hand down my face and grimace at the smell of horse manure, grapevines, and gunpowder—Mom would have a heart attack if she knew I spent all day shooting pegs and riding around on horseback *with a boy*. "Remember when she hid a metal spoon in the dish and then blamed me when the microwave exploded because I '*should have looked*' first. As in, she expected me to check if there was a utensil hidden in the curry." I throw my hands up, exasperated. "That woman is trying to kill me, Mathijs."

My home looms closer, and so does the impending contact with the woman who spawned me.

"Your mother will *not* kill you." He rubs my thigh, turning the control slightly. "She might lock you in a cell, but she won't kill you."

I hit his chest. "Not helping." I check the time and shake my head. "It's almost five o'clock now, so Mom's soul will be crawling out of hell and back into her body right about now. I haven't heard from her in twenty-six hours. *Twenty-six*." I hold up my cell. It's probably her new record. "I'm tempted to get my phone checked to see if it's broken. That's the only plausible explanation."

"Maybe, just *maybe*, she might be easing off your back."

I look his way for a moment before barking out a laugh.

"That woman has been on my ass since the moment I came out of the womb and everyone realized that the scans lied, and I am *very* much female."

A woman means something completely different in Western society. It doesn't matter that I was born on American soil; as far as Mom is concerned, we're still in India, and my life dreams are a personal offense to her.

The headphones crackle as Mathijs provides a string of information to traffic control as we close in on my house.

"You know..." Mathijs's full lips tip up into a grin as he gradually lowers us to the ground. "I could always propose. They can't get rid of me then, Zal."

"You're still the wrong-colored skin for my parents' tastes."

He knows it too.

Platinum blond hair, green eyes, and pale skin? On no planet would my parents think that's a suitable match for their daughter. The fact that his family could afford to surprise their son with a quarter million dollar present for his sixteenth birthday doesn't mean much to them either.

If they knew the true extent of what his family is into... I wouldn't put it past them to send Gaya and me to India.

"You know I don't want any of that until I finish college. It'll be the biggest *fuck you* to her if I get a degree *and* a man."

Mom's options for us are either doctor, lawyer, engineer, or housewife. Her preference would be the latter. My brother, Gadin, however, can be whatever he wants. He could say that he wants to be a princess, and Mom would break her back sewing

4

him the perfect gown.

Mathijs's hand moves from my lap, and I instantly miss the touch. Guilt gnaws at my insides as I glance at him, wondering if I'll be able to see the frustration bubbling inside. He hates that we have to keep our relationship a secret just so my parents don't find out and ship me off to a boarding school.

"You could just say 'fuck you' and move out now," he says as if it's the simplest solution. As supportive and understanding as he is about my family issues, he'll never really get it because he loves his parents, and they love him back. "You know my mom would cry happy tears if you stayed with us before we head to college."

He also wouldn't understand the issues of his suggestion. Moving out would mean saying goodbye to my parents and their bank account. I'm not bright enough to get a scholarship, and I haven't been working. My savings will hardly get me far.

Mathijs could cover my entire tuition four times over, and it wouldn't dent his account. But an innate part of me wants to prove to my mother that I don't need a man to survive.

My parents are still my meal ticket, and they have connections I'll need if I want to be successful in my career. If I didn't need them for anything, I wouldn't have been hiding my relationship with Mathijs since I was fourteen.

"They'll come around eventually," I respond with a sigh, checking my phone again.

I jolt as the landing skids hit the ground, narrowly avoiding the gilded water fountain at the front of my mid-century modern mansion.

My heart beats erratically as we land, and I notice all the lights that are on in our house. Is Gaya throwing a party again? The last time she did that, Mom slapped her with a slipper so hard, she had the shoe imprinted on her skin for days.

So did I for not stopping Gaya.

"Whose car is that?" Mathijs nods toward the Maserati parked by the house as he turns the engines and rotor off.

I don't think any of Gaya's friends own that type of car. The majority of them aren't even old enough to drive yet. Maybe one of them has an older boyfriend?

Mathijs shakes his head when the curtains ripple. "Your sister is just begging to get in trouble."

I make a noncommittal sound as I push the door open and jump onto the ground. Mathijs is beside me in an instant, closing the door for me and intertwining our fingers. He gives them a comforting squeeze that does nothing to soothe my unsettled nerves.

"I can stay over tonight and help with whatever mess Gaya and her friends make," he offers, then winks, nudging my side. "I'll be your bodyguard, baby. I'll protect you from drunk teenage girls."

I nod, but something feels wrong about the situation. There's no music or high-pitched giggling. It's too still.

My phone vibrates with an incoming text, and I read Gaya's message.

Gaya: Brace yourself. Tell your man to
run while he can.

The air catches in my throat when the next text comes in.

Gaya: They're back.

Blood rushes from my face.

I whirl toward Mathijs and snatch my hand away, hoping to every divine being there is that my parents somehow missed the helicopter landing in their driveway. "You need to go," I hiss.

His face falls as he stiffens, glancing around before dropping his gaze to the wide gap I've placed between us. "What's wrong?"

I stumble back, my throat closing. If my sister's right, I have to salvage this somehow. Maybe Mom didn't see us holding hands. Maybe she just got home and was in the shower so she didn't hear the commotion. "Gaya said they're—"

"*Zalak.*"

I freeze.

Shit. Shit. Shit.

My knuckles turn white as I spin toward her voice.

Mom stands at the front door, deathly still as she takes in every inch of me, burning holes through any semblance of armor I thought I might have. The disdain for me is as clear as day as she scrutinizes my mud-stained jeans and the fur covering my ripped shirt. Mathijs sports the same look as me.

The venomous scowl she cuts his way could kill a lesser man. But he doesn't back down. No. He does the opposite. He stands right beside me, too close for anyone to pass us off as *just friends*.

Papa appears in the doorway, holding up a phone to his ear and saying words I can't quite make out. He waves in the direction of the helicopter, shaking his head.

"Please leave," I whisper, hoping Mathijs hears my distress.

"Get inside. *Now*," Mom grounds out.

I move to step forward, but my boyfriend stops me with a hand around my arm.

"Leave, Mathijs." He doesn't let me yank my arm back, so I try again, shooting frantic looks back at my parents. "You're making it worse."

He ignores my pleas, looking at me with the same desperation that I feel. "Zal—"

"Get out of here."

"I'm not letting you deal with this alone. We'll tell her together." He attempts to interlock our fingers, but I scramble out of reach. If I can make him leave, maybe Mom's fury won't be as bad. I'll be able to salvage the situation.

"This is my problem to fix."

But as my gaze slams with Mom's, I realize there's no *fixing* this. She raised me better than to hope she could change. The only truth she'll ever believe is the one she told herself.

Mathijs curses at his phone. "Fuck, it's my dad." He ends the call and turns back to me, trying to close the distance between us when all I can do is inch back. "I'm not going anywhere. I promised you that you'll never have to do anything alone. *This* falls under that promise."

"*Zalak*," my father warns, making me flinch.

Mathijs narrows his eyes at my reaction. "Zal—"

"No, Mathijs." Panic bubbles up my throat. What if Mom doesn't let me have access to my savings account? I've relied on my parents for everything and they might take it away. What if she locks me in my room or takes it out on Gaya? What if she manages to get into my laptop and withdraws my college acceptance?

I have to do something. Anything.

I'll keep seeing Mathijs in secret. Tell Mom whatever she wants to hear. I have to *make this right*.

I can feel my parents' presence behind me, waiting by the door, more impatient by the second.

"Just leave!" I growl. Tears sting my eyes and my lungs scream louder than my racing pulse. The more he says, the worse it will be for me. "Please."

His phone lights up again with another call from his father that he ignores, then he grabs my arm. "Only if you promise to call me after."

"We'll see."

My stomach sinks from the hurt that flashes across his eyes. "Zal—"

"*Leave.*"

9

I can barely make out his face through my blurring vision. I blink my tears away as quickly as I can because my mother will prey on any kind of weakness, using it as a weapon to tell me all the ways I'm a disappointment to my family.

"Please," I whisper.

Mathijs lets me go. For some reason, it's like a part of my shattered heart breaks off and crumbles into dust. An open wound for my mother to prod at. He doesn't walk away. Instead, he watches me leave. Back turned on him. Steps heavy and soul aching. This feels like a goodbye.

The walk to the front door seems to stretch for miles. The crescent moons I've dug into my palms do nothing to ground me to Earth. It's like I'm walking to my slaughter.

Neither of my parents says anything as I walk inside, boots echoing on the tile. Trembling, I struggle to remove my shoes under the weight of their burning stare. The silence is always the worst. It means she's stewing. It means she's concocting a way to make me suffer for the crime of attempting to live outside of her control.

"Stand straight," Mom whispers in Hindi, poking my back. "Greet them, then say you'll return shortly."

"Who?" My voice comes out hoarse. The pristine white walls are closing in.

She doesn't respond, letting Papa lead the way through the foyer and toward the living area. I trail behind numbly, Mom hot on my heels with her long nails scraping my ribs through the thin fabric of my shirt.

Papa plasters on a forced smile as he turns toward the living room, holding his hand out to me. "My apologies. This is our daughter Zalak."

I hesitate before accepting it, and Mom takes it as a sign to shove me forward. I almost stumble as I approach Papa's side, only to find three people have risen to their feet alongside my brother.

It physically pains me to pull my lips into a smile, but I do it because Mom's punishment will only get worse if I don't pretend that everything is all sunshine and roses. The man who looks about my father's age steps forward first, offering me his hand in greeting.

"Madhav," he says. When I shake his hand, he muses, "Firm grip."

I sweeten my smile at the patronizing compliment, and shake the other person's hand. He's younger than the first. They almost look like the exact same person, just aged down about twenty years.

"Vatsa," he says.

The woman who I assume is his mother places her hands together and nods her head. I return the gesture.

The younger man unabashedly scans my body from head to toe, then cocks his head as if he hasn't decided whether he approves or not.

I quickly motion to my clothes, wanting to get rid of the family's assessment. "Sorry for this. I was out gardening," I lie. "I'll just go clean up first."

I hightail it out of the room, holding my breath to see whether Mom will follow or save the abuse for once the guests leave. The answering pad of footsteps brings a fresh wave of anxiety. I just can't win.

"Kitchen." Mom's voice echoes through the hallway.

There's no point fighting it. The sooner I do as she says, the sooner I can get this over with. I can't stop my skin from turning cold and clammy as my cheeks heat, ready for the oncoming tears that will be shed once I'm alone in my room.

Our footsteps echo against the tile floor, and a cold sweat breaks along my skin. I stand behind the kitchen island so Mom doesn't see me wringing my hands.

She opens the closest drawer to her and pulls out a letter, then places it on the counter between us. I lean closer to read it, and everything in me turns cold.

"Where did you find that?" My lungs seize as I glance at the college acceptance letter I never told her about. "Did you go through my room?"

Fuck.

Fuck.

"You weren't home," Mom says.

Of course she did.

Of course she fucking did. Why am I not surprised? I got complacent. It's been a year since she's looked through my phone; I don't know why I thought she might respect my space and privacy.

I can't keep living on eggshells.

She wasn't meant to find out like this—it's bad enough that I'm planning on moving out to study in a different state. The fact that I'm going to study political science... I was going to tell her next week once I found out if I managed to get the scholarship grant.

"That doesn't mean you can go through my room!"

Mom slaps her hand on the table then points at me. "Do not raise your voice at me. You're lucky I didn't get rid of you as a child." I choke back a sob. It isn't the first time she's said it, and I doubt it'll be the last time. It doesn't make it hurt any less. "I wish I did, when you're shaming our family by being a whore."

"I'm not a—"

"You dare speak back to me?" She raises her voice a decibel below a scream. "All you do is hurt me. I raised you, fed you, gave you a roof over your head. You think I had to do that? You think I have to live with an ungrateful daughter who lies just as much as she breathes."

"Mom, please," I beg. I wish she could be reasonable for at least two minutes so she can hear me out. "I wanted to tell you about Mathijs, but you're so unreasonable."

"And this?" Mom snatches the piece of paper off the table and waves it, crinkling the paper. "Political science?"

"I want to be a journalist," I say meekly.

"No one likes an opinionated woman." She scoffs as if my existence is more offensive than my response. "How do you think you're going to find a good husband?"

"Mathijs has been by my side for years. He wants me to do

whatever will make me happy—"

"Someone like him could never actually want you."

"He loves me," I insist. Her words hurt just as much as she intended them to. He *does* love me, but how long will that love last until he's tired of waiting for me to find myself? *Free* myself from my parents' hold.

"He'll grow up. Boys his age are young and immature; they don't know what they want or what's good for them. Once he comes to his senses, he'll realize that it isn't you." She shakes her head. "I have never trusted you because you don't know how to say no. My worries are correct. He's a bad influence on you. Sneaking out. Lying. Sleeping around. Tarnishing our name. This?"

She tears the letter in two. Then rips it up all over again until there's nothing but tiny pieces of paper that she lets fall onto the floor. Each one that lands feels like another part of my future being ripped away from me.

College.

A career of my choosing.

Mathijs.

Freedom.

"I'm doing you a favor." Mom sneers at the shredded letter. "You never would have made it far."

It takes everything in me not to drop to my knees and put it back together. "Why do you hate me so much?"

"*Beti*," Papa warns. *Daughter*.

I whip my attention toward him, unsure when he came into

the kitchen. Sometimes his presence instills hope in me that I'll have someone in my corner. But one look at him tells me I'm all alone in this.

"You're under my roof, and you dare insult me like this?" Mom hisses.

Gaya appears at the threshold, wide eyes darting between her and me. She looks showered and refreshed, like Mom just told her about the guests as well. I stiffen when her girlfriend, Amy, shows up behind her, grasping her elbow like she has any hope of stopping Gaya if she gets started.

Mom doesn't notice their arrival, continuing with her spiel. "If I hated you, I would have sent you to Mumbai where I'd never have to see your face. I sacrificed my happiness for you. I spent years finding you a suitable match, and all you've done is disrespect our family and his."

I blink. "His?"

Who is—

"The man in the living room."

No. *No.*

"Our families have agreed that it is a suitable match," Papa says, making me reach for the edge of the counter to hold myself up.

No, no, no. I know nothing about him. What if he doesn't let me study? What if his mom is just like mine? All my life she's been training me to be the right person for someone else. I just want to be my own person. Make my own decisions. Lead a path that I've set for myself.

15

"No, you cannot *make her* marry anyone," Gaya argues. I shoot her a look to get her to shut up, but she ignores it, holding her head up higher. It's my job to stand up for her, not the other way around.

"But you might have ruined everything already." Mom scowls.

"You're being ridiculous."

"*Gaya*," I warn, but I know it's useless. She usually has Papa in her court, so she can get away with almost everything... except the fact that she's only interested in other women.

"He has to be, what? Midthirties?" she keeps going, getting closer to Mom like it might drive her message home. "He's already graying. Are you crazy?"

I clap my hand over my mouth when a *smack* sounds through the room. Gaya's body swings to the side from the force of Mom's slap, then she whirls toward me before I can make it to my sister's side, holding her hand up as a silent threat that she will hit me too if I interfere.

"You are going to go upstairs, shower, dress nicely, and you will *never* see that boy again. You are going to greet your future husband, and once he leaves, you are going to withdraw all your college applications, and you *will* be a good wife."

Tears spill down my cheeks. "And if I do none of those things?"

"Then you will no longer have a family."

CHAPTER 1

ZALAK

Ten years later

I might kill a man tonight.

I've fallen in the ring before. Broken bones, spilled my own blood on the concrete floor, yet I've never taken my last breath in front of people betting on my demise.

The roar of the crowd vibrates through the walls and rattles the metal lockers. Incomprehensible jeering, intermittent cheers, and collective gasps fill the space of the decrepit room. Life exists beyond the stained four walls surrounding me. But here, with the yellowing plaster and cracked basin, it feels like a place where people come to die.

Every time I sit on a bench, wrapping my hands with gauze, bandages, and tape, I picture myself stopping someone's heart with a single strike. I imagine the crowd will explode with delight at the sight of death and the ensuing riches. I thought my mother's wrath and my father's disappointment were the worst I could endure. I was wrong.

This? There are no words to describe the seventh level of hell I've found myself in. I didn't fall from grace; I was ripped away from it. Two and a half years ago, my wings were torn and my armor turned to dust. All within three days.

Flexing my fists, I focus on the wooden door. Any second, there will be a knock. At any moment my heart will remember it isn't dead, and my brain will feel something other than oblivion.

I trace the scorpion tattoo hidden beneath the wrapping on my hand, with a pincer reaching for my thumb and pointer finger. Parts of it are still raised above the skin despite the months that have passed since I got it. My sister has an exact replica of it on her ribs.

Had.

What's left of it is ash in the Atlantic Ocean. Along with the debris from the plane crash. Gaya finally got the freedom she wanted.

I had told her the heavy-handed tattoo would look ridiculous against the patchwork of all the fine line art she etched into her body the second I got her away from our parents. But she flipped me off, called me an idiot for not appreciating the reference she was making, and got it anyway.

A chorus of cries and shouts blare through the warehouse, echoing through the concrete corridors. It sends a ripple of anticipation down my spine as I roll my shoulders, stretch out the tension coiling my muscles tight.

Three consecutive knocks boom through the room. "We're ready."

Two words and my blood soars. Two words and I feel alive again. Adrenaline pumps through my veins and howls in my ears. My skin prickles with warmth at the impending feel of skin against skin. We all have to get our kicks somehow.

Gone is the thrill of falling out of helicopters. There's no going back to the life I had before I failed my sister and my team.

Cheap thrills and blood money are my penance.

Unclasping my necklace, I press the gold coin pendant to my lips and try to remember the last time I saw Gaya wearing it, but the picture is all faded and murky now. I'm losing her more and more every day.

I tuck the necklace into the pocket of my pants and check that my dog tags are there. The wooden bench creaks as I rise. I have to adjust my sports bra again because the band has loosened after one too many wears, and my wallet is far too thin.

I stop at the end of the hall and peer out at the masses congregating around a center point. The exhilaration in the air is palpable.

The place reeks of cigarettes, piss, beer, and stale body odor, just like every other club I've ever been to these past two years. As disgusting as it is, the foul smell centers me until I notice every single minute detail of my surroundings. The weight of my leather boots. The pins holding my braid to my scalp. The woman in gray picking the pockets of unsuspecting men. Five exits: the one I'm in, the two roller doors, one at eleven o'clock, and the last at three.

Men and women from all trenches of society are here too. The Wall Street types, gang bangers, made men, and the unassuming neighbors next door.

Another city. Another fight club. Another chance to die a soldier's death. All guts and no glory.

"Ladies and gents, we've got a crowd favorite up next." The commentator's voice booms through the megaphone, barely drowning out the sounds of excited chatter. He turns around on his stool to suck in the entire audience. "Five foot seven, with six consecutive knockout wins, and Colorado's newest fighter." The six knockouts happened months ago, and I haven't had a decent win in over seven weeks. And unless there's a stack of cash in my hands at the end of the night, I'm losing my apartment tomorrow. "She's venomous, she's a striker, and she's out for blood. Give it up for the *Deathstalkerrr*!"

The room erupts into shouting and screaming. I glance down at the tattoo on my hand. The deathstalker scorpion.

Sergeant of the 75th Ranger Regiment. Eleven Bravo. Special Operations Forces.

Codename: *Scorpion*.

The sound slams into me when I shove the door open and stalk toward the center of the warehouse. People part like the sea, giving me a direct line to the makeshift ring. The rush of power that comes from the simple act used to make me heady, but it's been a long time since the attention of the crowd has done more than spike my anxieties from being the center of attention.

Stacks of green are passed around in exchange for tokens that are quickly tucked away into pockets. The guy uses a marker on each note to check that it isn't a counterfeit before moving to the next person to repeat the same process. I'm going to make someone rich tonight.

Some men leer, others salivate at the prospect of thickening their wallets. But some? They look like they can't wait for me to die. It's a look I became familiar with the second my mother birthed a daughter and not another son.

As I close in on the empty, circular space in the middle of the room, the noises drown beneath my racing pulse. Crimson and brown splatters decorate the gray concrete floor, working their way into every crevice and pore, leaving a near permanent mark of another fighter.

I fold my hands behind my back once I reach the middle of the ring, keeping my gaze directly on the commentator. I never asked who I'll be facing. I never want to know more details than how much I'll make if I get the other person on the ground. Or under it.

The commentator drones on about my opponent, but I can't make sense of his words when his deep brown eyes meet mine for half a second too long. My lungs constrict and my ears ring with the sound of a phantom explosion. *I'm back there*. My skin crawls with the imaginary feeling of having shrapnel piercing my flesh, as I watch my best friend's eyes grow cold and vacant as he bleeds out onto the asphalt.

TJ needs help. I need to call for backup. But I can't move, there's something on top of me. I have to help—

I suck in a sharp breath and snap my head up at the commentator when he says the two syllables that turn my blood cold "... let's give up for H-Brawn."

Fuck.

Fuck.

Screams erupt through the room, piercing through my eardrums as a brick wall pushes through the crowd without a care for all the men and women he bulldozes over.

My breathing staggers as I eye him up. All three hundred pounds of him. Bald with a deranged stare. Brawn's lips peel back into a smile that's all teeth.

I'm screwed. I've taken men his size in a fight before, but my body takes this exact moment to send a searing shot of pain through my foot. I need treatment I can't afford, and it gets worse every time my brain thinks I'm back there. The sound of everyone betting in his favor has sweat building between my shoulders, sticking my ripped tank top to my skin.

It's getting incrementally harder to pull air into my lungs. If I tap out, I'll never get into a fight again, and the feeling of fists against skin is the only thing getting me through. My knuckles turn white as I stare H-Brawn back down.

Tension winds my muscles tighter as H-Brawn stalks forward. I try cataloging all his weak spots: throat, the slight lag in his left foot, his speed, raisin-sized balls—cheap shots will still pay rent.

He looks me dead in the eye as he stretches his neck from side to side, cracking his knuckles. "Hope you said your goodbyes, Princess."

My lip twitches. No, I didn't get the chance to. They died before I could.

Like a barbarian, he throws his arms up in the air and roars. The audience eats it up, matching the sound with feral cries and hoots as he beats his chest. All the while, I stay perfectly still with my legs shoulder width apart and my hands folded behind my back.

"Get your bets in—my money's on H-Boy." The commentator snickers into the megaphone.

I don't even dignify his comment with a glare, instead pretending like the muscles in my foot aren't cramping under my weight. Two and a half years later, and there's still no escaping the traumas of my last mission.

"Who's ready?" Another chorus of cheers spreads through the room, and H-Brawn rolls his shoulders before raising his arms into a fighting stance. "*Three, two, one... fight.*"

The last word doesn't make it out before he barrels for me. I drop onto one knee at the very last second and kick my leg out. His lower stomach collides with my boot, and agony thunders up my leg, sending bolts of pain up my spine and over my skin as if I'm back to bleeding out a couple of feet away from the burning armored car.

He grunts at the impact, buckling over ever so slightly as he reaches for the foot I can barely feel because of the damaged nerve. I manage to escape his grasp to weakly bury my heel into the soft area on the inside of his legs, just above his knees. The move makes him stagger forward, and I leap up onto my good foot to smash the hard surface of my palm against his nose.

The crowd goes wild as his head whips back and blood spurts out of the crooked line of his nose. Any sense of triumph is short-lived when his fists knock my raised hands aside and clock me in the jaw.

Both of my feet weaken, threatening to send me tumbling. I manage to hold myself up despite the agony. Pain blooms across my cheek. Blood coats my tongue.

I'd be a damn liar if I said there isn't something glorious about external pain. It's liberating and self-destructive. Grounding me and setting me over the edge.

I don't notice the second hit until the air *whooshes* out of my lungs, and I fold over.

This is the type of crap that happens when I never get my ass out of bed: I get weak. Worse, I get slow. The people I served with would be appalled if they saw what I've become.

I slam my fists against his ear and narrowly dodge his next attack, sidestepping and ducking over and over before snagging his rib with my elbow. H-Brawn's blow hits me right against my mouth. Blood spurts from the split in my lip, and I bite back a cry as I pivot on my bad foot, unleashing another pathetic kick to his side.

We go back and forth for minutes, with me spending more time dodging strikes than landing one. But everything I do makes him increasingly pissed off, and his hits seem to do increasingly more damage. Blood mixes with sweat, dripping down his forehead and torso in streams of pink. If my leg wasn't playing up, I could climb onto his shoulder and bring him down onto the floor, then try to dislocate his shoulder or break his elbow.

For a split second, I swear my eyes lock on a pair of striking green ones. *Mathijs*. It's gone the instant H-Brawn clocks me in the ribs.

God, I shouldn't have come back to this city. I knew it would mess with my head, but I came back anyway. I don't want to be back here among the ghosts of my past, but I couldn't stay in California seeing Gaya in every corner of the room.

Closing the gap, I lift my knee to shove it in H-Brawn's gut, but his arms encircle me before I can, lifting me up and slamming me onto the concrete. Pain radiates from every bone in my body, and a sickening *crack* echoes through my skull from the impact.

Cotton-wrapped knuckles meet my cheek, sending white dots scattering over my vision, blurring his vicious face as another strike hits my brow. Meaty fingers wrap around my throat, cutting off all oxygen. White spots turn black, and my lungs burn as if I've been left for dead at the bottom of the ocean. I try breaking his hold, twisting his wrists away, clawing at his skin, and bucking his weight off. Nothing works.

This time, when my ears ring, it's a different type of siren than the one I heard while I had lain helpless and watched my friends die. Because this time, it sounds like a melody. A call from the beyond, beckoning me to fall over the edge and succumb to the darkness.

They say time heals all wounds. That as the days go on, you'll stop grieving the ones you love. But I don't want time. I refuse to sit around waiting for the pain to hurt a little less, for the tears to burn a little softer. I want to beat the emotions out of me until it stops hurting, and I go back to being the type of woman my sister could be proud of.

Some call my addiction to the ring having pain I can control.

I call it weaponizing death.

I've long since made peace with the grim reaper. He can take me whenever he wants. If today's my day, I'll welcome his cold embrace with open arms. At least if I die in the ring, I'll get to feel alive one last time.

So when everything goes black, I don't fight it.

CHAPTER 2

ZALAK

O xygen slams into me all at once. I buckle over, gasping for air, choking on each breath through my bruising esophagus. Rolling onto my elbows, I try to steady my pulse and focus on filling my lungs, but I can barely manage the simple task. I spit blood onto the floor covered in fresh crimson droplets, then drag my hand across my eye to stop the liquid from impairing my vision even more.

H-Brawn's blurry figure circles the ring with his arms up.

No. *No.* Fuck.

I bite back a groan as I pull myself up onto my feet and try not to limp on my walk of shame back to the locker. But everyone can see it. There's no denying that I can barely put any weight on my foot, or that I'm practically dragging it across the ground.

I can feel all their eyes on me, their disappointment and smug victory. But it's nothing compared to the next twelve hours if I don't fork up some cash.

Red rims my vision, whether from the blood or from rage, I'm not sure. My bruised body protests against my movements, screaming at me to sit down. I slam the door to the locker room open and stagger inside.

"Fuck," I growl, slapping the wall. The sound vibrates through the room, followed by another *bang* when I level my fists with the metal lockers.

No money. No health insurance. No fucking place to live after tomorrow.

Pathetic. Just like my parents always thought I was.

I don't care if I'm on the street or living off food scraps. I'm not going to go crawling to my brother for a handout when he always took our parents' side. Now Gaya is dead because they convinced her to visit our relatives in India, and her corpse is somewhere in the Atlantic Ocean, rotting alongside the parents who never gave a shit about us and two hundred other people.

I haven't got many things—most of what my sister owned stayed with her wife, Amy—so I can rent a storage room and set up a tent in the forest until I figure it out. Plus, there's no way I can share a space with someone, especially if I'm in a mood. Amy should be fine if I don't send her any money for the next few weeks.

I'm just so fucking tired of everything. I'm sick of moving. I'm sick of living like this.

Yanking the towel off the bench, I hobble over to the sink to dampen the material, then attempt to wipe as much blood off my face as I can. The cut on my forehead and lip doesn't let up, leaking crimson from the gaping wound.

I grit my teeth as I press the towel to my forehead, letting the metallic coat my taste buds, as I rummage around for my first aid kit. Red stains the Band-Aid I press onto my forehead within seconds. It needs stitches, but I can't afford to get them.

My busted lip isn't doing much better. It's soaking a separate piece of cloth that I'm holding between my teeth. Every part of my body screams in pain as I drop down onto the bench to unwrap my knuckles and hiss as I shove my arms into a hoodie, leather jacket, then backpack. Clasping my helmet beneath my chin, I give the room a passing glance before limping out into the hall, taking the back exit to avoid facing the crowds.

I should be tracking down the promoter to get me in another fight, but I'm in no condition to get in the ring for another few weeks. Hell, I haven't been in the right condition for months since I drunkenly fell down the stairs one night. My foot has been making me pay double time for it ever since.

I can barely smell the crisp night air as I limp toward my bike. It'll be a miracle if I make it to my apartment in one piece. Every breath hurts, and I'm going to have to rely on my right leg for the drive. I'd rather risk getting into an accident than call down a taxi to take me home—not that I can afford it anyway.

Biting down on the towel, I throw my leg over my motorbike and slump down onto the metal to catch a moment's reprieve from the pins and needles rendering my left foot numb and aching.

The bike rumbles to life beneath me, and I flinch, blinking back the image of the roaring flames coming from the armored car. My arms shake as I grip the handles. I don't let myself think about my exhaustion as I peel away from the park and make my way to my apartment. Probably for the last time.

I'm not entirely sure how I made it home, but I know I did it, driving on autopilot until I'm struggling up the stairs with my helmet tucked beneath my arm and my hand in a death grip around the railing.

I lean half my weight against the wall, focusing on the dirty linoleum floors beneath me as I lift my knee higher than necessary to stop from dragging my foot. The edges of my vision blur and my head swims. Blood trickles out of the Band-Aid and down the side of my temple, as well as from the middle of my lip.

When was the last time I ate a proper meal? Do I even have any painkillers left for my foot?

Fuck. I should have died in that explosion too.

"Sergeant Bhatia."

I snap upright, flooded with a sudden burst of energy. No one has called me that in two and a half years, and I'm sure no one from the club knows I'm ex-military.

My vision focuses on the man leaning against the door to my apartment, and a wave of emotions crashes through me.

No. He isn't meant to know that I'm back, let alone know

where I live.

I always thought I'd be in a casket the next time I saw the boy I left behind. But there he is—Mathijs Halenbeek. Even more beautiful than the last time I saw him. Age has done him wonders. He no longer has a layer of baby fat concealing the sharp edges of his bone structure. The boy I knew held wonder in his green eyes, and his pale skin radiated sunlight. But the man before me has lost the light; sunken cheeks and chiseled jaw, sharp eyes, and platinum hair that's two shades lighter than I remember.

Hollow. Haunted.

Like a ghost.

Still, even under the dim hallway light, he's the most beautiful man I've ever seen. He's out of place in this decrepit apartment, wearing his three-piece suit and woolen coat that fits his slender waist to perfection.

Just looking at him hurts. I lost him and my parents in a single night. Then, I lost my sister and my best friend within a week. The only person who survived the last ten years is him. Even then, it looks like every day that passes, his grip on life has been weakening too.

"I'm not a sergeant anymore," I grumble through the cloth, dropping my head to avoid him seeing more of my ruined face.

I shoulder by him to get to my door, but he blocks the way. Irritation slices through me, and I have to stop myself from lashing out at him for something that he has no fault in. I've lost everything, and his presence is only acting as a reminder that I've

31

failed every single person in my life.

I yank the cloth out of my mouth. "What are you doing here, Mathijs?"

He looks at me for a long moment, dragging his gaze over the cuts on my face, my disheveled braid, down to the way I'm holding my foot. He catalogs every inch of me as if he's waited a lifetime to do it, and he has no intention of rushing.

The weight of his simple gesture crushes my chest, making me feel seen in a way I haven't felt in almost a decade. It's different from the leering I got when I was a new recruit, or when I'm in the ring. Those looks came with the intention of *taking*. Mathijs's look is calculating with the air of something warmer. Something heavy.

It almost tastes like longing.

For the first time since I stepped on the bus to get shipped off to training, I can't help wondering how I look through his eyes. Messy and bloody, ashen from too many days spent in a bed surrounded by empty bottles. I'm almost tempted to run my hand over my head to flatten down any loose strands.

Does he see Zalak, the girl he once loved, or Zalak, the one who let him down?

When he breaks the silence, a part of me tears in two because I never thought a dream could become reality.

"Sergeant Zalak Bhatia of the 75th Regiment. Thirty-three confirmed kills." He leans against the wall, crossing his arms and long legs. His voice lacks the softness I grew up falling asleep to the sound of. It's clinical and monotonous. I'd think he didn't care for any of it if it weren't for the way his eyes light up with pride. "By twenty-five, you set the record as the woman with the highest confirmed deaths outside of wartime. You were commended for executing a confirmed kill at thirteen hundred meters during your deployment in the Middle East—another record for women."

"That's confidential." No one knows that. I was discharged on grounds of injury and PTSD, and everything me and my team did was sealed shut.

"You executed a surgical high priority Special Operations Raid in Senegal before you were discharged."

I suck in a sharp breath. If I hadn't swapped seats with TJ on the way back to base, he'd be alive, and I'd be the one six feet under alongside my sister. It was a standard intel gathering mission. No one was meant to die. But I didn't see the group waiting for us up on the cliff. No one did.

"You moved here six months ago and you're in need of a job," Mathijs continues.

"Get out of my building." God, it sounds just like the last words I said to him.

Mathijs's eyebrows twitch like he's trying to hide the fact that he's realized the same thing. "Let me rephrase. I need security—a bodyguard, if you will—and you need employment." He glances at my front door where an eviction notice is taped to it. "And a roof over your head." His eyes drop from the saturated Band-Aid on my forehead to my drop foot. "And medical assistance."

"I'm fine."

He lowers his shoulder and clasps his hands behind his back, a subtle upward tilt to his lips as if he knows he's going to get the answer he wants tonight. "I offer my staff a 401(k), health insurance, and free accommodation. Tell me, how much would you make in a fight?"

"Enough."

Nowhere near enough to survive off or have any savings, especially if I'm sending money to help Amy finish her degree now that Gaya isn't here to support her. And I don't exactly have any savings.

I hate that he knows how desperate I am. That he knows the state of my life when I know nothing about him beyond the fact that I'm not the only one who lost family.

I don't want to live in a fucking tent. I don't want Amy's things to be in storage. I don't want to keep feeling pain in my foot all because I don't have the means to get it treated. Sure, I had surgery on it after the accident. But no one has looked at it since. This country doesn't give a shit about its veterans.

"Before the accident, you could disable someone twice your size within forty-eight seconds. You graduated top in your class. Your shots hit more than they miss. Would you like me to go into detail about all the successful extractions and hits you did?"

"I'm still not interested." If I have to work security, I'll do it for someone other than my ex.

I limp around him and use the door handle as support while I fumble for the key.

34

"The starting salary is ninety thousand for someone of your expertise."

I'm interested. "Fine."

The response comes out quicker than I intend it to. Money like that could wipe out Amy's student loan and some of her medical bills.

I make the mistake of glancing up at Mathijs to find his lips stretched into a half smile. Still as arrogant as ever. "You can move in tomorrow and start work in two weeks. I'll send you the address."

"I have an apartment."

He nods. "Until tomorrow, I believe."

I narrow my eyes. That's not on the notice taped to my door. "How do you get all your information?"

I don't know why I bother asking. His family's hedge fund business is only a front; their real money comes from the underbelly of this city. Mathijs's father wouldn't have been impressed if he knew that his son told his fifteen-year-old girlfriend that their family is in a gang-like secret society.

"You and I aren't the same kids we used to be. In our line of work, the better we are at something, the more enemies we have." He steps forward as if he wants to touch me. "Zalak..." I turn away, knowing the next words that will come out of his mouth. "I'm sorry to hear about your sister and your team. I'm... I'm here for you if you need a—"

"I don't need your handouts," I snap when pain spikes up my leg. Fuck, I need to sit.

It's not exactly how I should be talking to my new boss or someone who is just trying to make my life better. I need a fucking seat and a drink. Which means I need him gone.

"You can say many things, but do not insult me by referring to yourself like that. I don't have a death wish, Zalak. If I wanted to open a charity, I am well capable of doing so."

"When did you become such an asshole?" I've always been one. The Mathijs I remember was the king of sugarcoating.

"When I lost the one thing that was important to me." His stare bores into me, picking apart every part of me that I've kept hidden away. "Take my condolences or don't. It's there for you either way."

I nod, swallowing the boulder that's lodged itself in my throat. "Thank you. And I'm... I'm sorry to hear about your parents." Taking a solidifying breath, I stand straighter. "I was on deployment, and I only found out about what happened two weeks after the funeral. I wish I could have attended. They... they were the parents I never had."

He gives me a sad smile. "You were the daughter they always wanted."

Tears sting my eyes, and I avert my attention to unlocking the door so he doesn't see how far I've fallen in the past decade. The lock clicks open and I inch the door wider to end the conversation.

Instead of staying put like a gentleman, the little shit barges past me and enters my apartment, switching on the lights as if he owns the place.

"I never invited you inside," I grind out, hating that he's seeing how pathetic my studio is. There's a beat-up double-seater couch, a coffee table with a thousand ring stains, and a duvet that should have made its way to the dump a long time ago. Other than a single photo frame of me, Gaya, and TJ next to the TV, nothing about the apartment seems like a home.

Despite how measly my living situation is, and how horrific I must look, he doesn't bat an eye, leaning against the kitchen counter with his arms crossed as if *I'm* the one intruding on his space. "Then tell me to leave."

I'd rather choke than say those specific words to him again.

I hobble inside, dump my helmet and backpack on the counter, then grab two bottles of beer from the fridge. He shakes his head at my offer, so I press one of the drinks against my swollen eye. The condensation mixes with the blood still trickling from my forehead and down my neck, but I try to play it off like I'm not about to lose my sanity and consciousness. I slump against the fridge, praying that my good leg doesn't give out on me too.

It takes longer than I care to admit to figure out that there's a red bag on the kitchen bench. It's a med kit.

A med kit that does not belong to me.

Did he know I was fighting tonight?

Mathijs nods toward the single dining chair. "Sit."

"I can deal with it myself." It isn't the first time I've had to treat cuts that needed stitches, antibiotics, and some damn good painkiller.

"You need stitches." He glances around, then opens one of the drawers and holds up the emergency sewing kit. Has he been here before? "Unless you want regular cotton sewn into your skin."

I narrow my eyes at him.

Fuck it. I'll comply only because I can't afford to replace my pillow and bedsheets.

The chair creaks beneath my weight, and it's sad that I have to hold back a sigh of relief.

"Do you have strong painkillers?" Mathijs asks, following behind me with the little med kit.

I crack open the beer bottle using the edge of the wooden table, then hold up the drink in answer.

The muscle in his jaw twitches, but he says nothing as I down two-thirds of it in one go. It tastes like flavored dirt, and the added metallic tang doesn't do it any favors.

Mathijs is methodical in the way he lays out his supplies, going so far as disinfecting the table before placing a sheet on it. The kit has everything he needs in it, from Panadol that he makes me take with water, to gauze, to tools he needs to stitch my forehead back together.

I have no way to prove it, or the words to ask, but I'm certain he planned for me to leave the ring broken. It's the only way to explain why he's carrying around the kit with him.

Slipping his hands into a pair of medical-grade gloves, he turns to me with a wipe and a cotton ball doused in iodine.

"This is going to hurt."

I lift a shoulder. "I'm used to it."

His jaw feathers again. I manage to hold back any reaction to the sting that hits my forehead beyond a shaky inhale. The burn is almost relaxing.

Controlled pain. It's the best kind.

I finish my drink off then start on the other as he grabs the threaded needle and a pair of forceps. My fingers curl around my seat, and I grunt when the point pierces my skin. He doesn't react, green eyes focused on my bleeding flesh, working quickly with practiced ease.

For the briefest moment, I can picture how he would light up every time he was around animals. If life gave him a family with different expectations, he'd be wearing scrubs and working as a vet, not wearing a suit, stitching someone up after an underground street fight.

I hiss when the needle punctures flesh again. "You know how to sew." Not a question, but something to fill the tense silence.

"You were slower than usual tonight."

My eyes snap up to his. "Than usual?"

Mathijs doesn't answer.

He's seen me fight? How many times? Have I become so far removed from reality that I've stopped doing a proper scan of the crowd? Fuck. What's the point of knowing where the exits are when I have no idea where the danger is?

Part of me wants to know why he hasn't approached me sooner. For years, I've known that there wouldn't be a day that I'm ready to face him after leaving him behind. Maybe he knows it too.

I jolt, not expecting the next stitch. Sucking in a sharp breath, I stare at the ground. "You haven't asked me why I left."

"I have many questions, *Lieverd*," he says softly. *Darling*. My breath catches. "That isn't the one that keeps me up at night."

Keeps. Not *kept*.

The boulder in my throat doubles in size and doesn't go away when I swallow.

Why did you leave without me? Why didn't you come to me first? Why haven't you contacted me over all these years? Why didn't you say goodbye?

This time, I say nothing.

I don't feel the last stitch or the tightening as he ties it off. The cool touch of an alcohol wipe feels a mile away, and I barely hear his final words to me or the creak of the floor with his departure.

Once the door closes behind him, I just sit there, on a threadbare chair in an empty beat-up apartment I'm going to lose, and I make peace with what I am. What I've always been. I ran from home and hid from the world when it got too hard. I've been running and rotting away ever since my world came crashing down.

I know the answer to the questions he never asked.

I'm a coward.

CHAPTER 3

MATHIJS

*E**arlier that day*

It's been over 3728 days since Zalak left.

Finally she's here. In my city. Right in my line of sight.

Zalak Bhatia. My little *Lieverd*. The girl I fell in love with before I even heard her voice. The girl I lost before I got a chance to say goodbye. No last kiss. No last touch. Nothing but silence.

Now I'm watching her get beaten within an inch of her life.

Golden brown skin bloody and bruised, her black hair whips from side to side with each move. I wince when the brute's fist collides with her jaw. It's hard to stomach, but I stay there, holding back a grimace every time a strike lands on her.

It isn't the first time I've seen her fight, and I doubt it will be the last. If I have any say in it, she'll never need to throw a punch again until her foot is all healed up and in a state where nobody can see her weakness.

"She's got good form and bad footwork," Sergei appraises beside me.

I nod. I wouldn't jump into a decision to hire her if my right-hand man and head of security thought I'd just be putting her life in danger. Her kill stats with a rifle speak for themselves. He needs to determine whether I'll be able to sleep peacefully at night, or if I'll be too busy worrying that she can't hold her own outside of a ring.

"She's already better than most of our men."

Never in a million years did I think I could say that *my* Zalak could take my own soldiers in a fist fight. Yet there she is, giving a man twice her size just as much hell. I just need to convince her that she doesn't need to live a life where she's spending her nights in an underground fighting ring just to survive.

Sergei scrutinizes her, leaning back against the wall that would dirty my coat in a way I have no interest in. "Fast. Decent hook. Mediocre recovery. I think she'll need minimal training once she fixes that foot of hers."

That sounds like approval to me.

Zalak needs medical treatment, and she's not going to get it even if a pile of cash drops on her lap and someone tells her she needs it.

I tried looking for her but she kept jumping from city to city, never staying in one place for too long, and always paying cash. I thought she might have been running from someone. It turns out she's just running from herself.

As horrific as it is to admit, I preferred it when she was serving in the military. At least then, I could check on her every day to see where she was stationed, what kind of missions she was being sent on, and gauge how she was by her and her team's reports. These past two years, the signs of life were few and far between. The videos I managed to get of her fights served as the only proof that she was still upright. Even then, I wasn't convinced she was.

Zalak's eyes might still be the same dark brown they've always been, but now they're empty, and it kills me that she's become nothing more than a ghost. I remember seeing pictures of her before her team was attacked. She used to be packed with muscle and exude power. Now she's little more than skin and bone.

All of that needs to change.

As soon as I found out she returned, nothing would have kept me away. It's taking me too long to figure out how to reel her in and get her within my grasp where she won't despise me for taking her in. She was mine before and it's time to make her mine again, because I was always hers. I have been since day one.

All it took was for someone to kill my bodyguard, and the idea fell right into my lap.

Zalak is stubborn and relentless. She hated being coddled, and I can only imagine how foreign it would be to have someone take care of her. It kills me to think how long she's been alone for. Suffering in silence because she thinks no one would be there to listen. I would've been there even if I had to crawl to get to her.

I may have needed to deal with the loss of my parents too, but the difference between us is that I had people around me to get me through. If it weren't for Sergei to keep the cogs ticking and to point me in the right direction, I doubt I would have made it out.

I had purpose and support. I want that for her too. She deserved the world back when she thought her parents ripped it away from her, and she deserved it when the people she loved were.

"Fucking hell," I mutter and look away when H-Brawn knocks her off her feet.

I train my eyes on Zalak's near lifeless form as the crowd goes wild. The monstrosity on legs roars, holding up both arms in victory. I roll my eyes. They're always so cringey when they win. The times I've seen Zalak victorious, she stretches her neck from side to side, then walks straight out of the ring like it's just another Thursday.

Only this time she can barely get herself up. Her bad leg trembles beneath her weight as she hobbles out. My blood rises three degrees from the jeers and leers thrown her way. I just want to run over and help her the rest of the way, but I know well enough that it's the worst possible thing I could do.

We hang back as the crowd readies for another round of bloodshed. Someone hands Sergei a pile of cash and I glare at him.

He shrugs, tucking his winnings into his jacket pocket. "The odds weren't in her favor."

I scoff, shaking my head as I head toward the exit. I put ten grand on her to win.

"Let's bring my girl home."

CHAPTER 4

ZALAK

Four Years Ago

"Make me a promise," I whisper loud enough that TJ—Tito Jimenez—can hear without giving away our position.

The desert heat chars my skin, and the sand beneath my stomach threatens to turn the both of us into steak. What I wouldn't give for an ice bath right now. And a decent meal. And a good bed.

The cement building stares back at me, taunting me with its empty windows. The nonexistent heat signature is like a gut punch to all the hours we've already spent scoping this place.

"Don't worry. If you get stung by a scorpion again, I'll name my sixthborn after you." He chuckles from beside me.

Not this again.

I pull the finger at him without compromising my position and hold on the sniper rifle. "Someone would need to be willing to sleep with you first before agreeing to spawn your offspring."

"I'll have you know that the ladies find me *extremely* charming." Fake offense drips from his tone.

"Your mom doesn't count."

"But my *abuela* does."

I huff out a laugh. "As soon as we get back to base, take a fucking shower. If they can't hear us, they'll sure as shit smell you."

"It's called pheromones."

Having a spotter is all fun and games until you're in the desert heat doing surveillance. Out of everything this job puts us through, this type of work is the worst. My main distraction comes down to my need to wash my stench off me.

An hour of this is fun.

Three is relaxing.

Six gets boring.

Eight is taxing.

Twelve? I'd be willing to kill TJ just to get out of here.

Shaking my head, I scope the parameter again. Like always, there's not a soul in sight at the abandoned compound. A warlord is allegedly residing here. Whoever gave us the info can eat shit if they intentionally fed us wrong intel.

Our instructions are to call it in if he's spotted, then hold position until backup arrives so we can bring him in dead or alive. But there's been absolutely zero fucking movement in five hours. The only live thing we've seen is a dog.

TJ and I think the intel is all shit. Until proven otherwise, the twelve hours we've been here will continue to stretch to sixteen until someone grants us the mercy of taking our place.

The winds are picking up, and the last thing I want is to be caught out in the desert with our dwindling supplies. And if there's a sandstorm? I'll personally escort us both to the gates of hell to get out of this shithole.

I radio in to the second location his wife allegedly lives at. "Anything?"

"A kid just showed up," Marks mutters. "No signs otherwise."

I grit my teeth just as the captain's voice rumbles through the headset. "Give it two more hours."

TJ sighs. "I need to take a leak."

Lovely.

Shuffling ensues beside me, and I glare at him when his ghillie suit slaps me in the face. He returns shortly after, and after an hour of silence, he says, "Want to play I-Spy?"

Whatever. What the fuck. Why not?

Our captain would be mortified if he knew what we're doing for the proceeding hour. After years of playing this game during stakeouts, we've gotten really good at mind fucking each other with the answer.

I spy with my little eye, something beginning with S.

Sand?

No. Stratosphere.

Can it be seen? No. Is it cause for ample bickering to pass the time? Yes.

I've had other spotters in the past, and TJ is the only one I've ever clicked with. Now we couldn't get rid of each other even if we tried.

"Meet at the pickup point at twenty-hundred hours," the captain finally says three hours later.

I glance at my watch. *Thank god*. It isn't so hot anymore, but the showers are calling my name.

"Copy that," TJ answers for me.

I wrap the towel around my body and squeeze out the excess water from my long hair, then get dressed into my clean uniform in case the captain decides he wants our asses back out there.

TJ walks out of the bathroom at the exact same time. A grin slashes across his face when he sees me, and he lifts up his arm to take a deep whiff of his armpits. "Smells like roses." He sighs dreamily.

I gag. "Disgusting."

"Nice and washed just for you, roomie."

My lips curl into a scowl as we both walk to the designated room I have the misfortune of sharing with him—as if spending fifteen hours with him wasn't enough time for us to bond. I love him, but I wouldn't mind some space every once in a while.

It's one of the smaller bases in this country, and our team is only meant to be here for a couple days. Because I'm the only woman in a ten-mile radius, they don't have the place to spare to let me bunk by myself, so they shoved me in with TJ and a sleep-talker.

My dog tags sway as we walk through the building to the rooms. Most of the soldiers have gone to bed already, so we sneak into our room without waking anyone. I slowly open the door and glance inside, but there's no one in our temporary stay. The third person we're rooming with must still be on a mission.

Unlucky for some.

We shuffle forward to switch on the lamp against the back wall.

"I'm fucked. If you start snoring, I'm covering your face with a pillow," TJ grumbles as he plops down onto the cot.

"Ditto." I copy what he does, except more eloquently.

I untie my boots and place them right next to my cot before lying down on the uncomfortable material. Reaching inside my pocket, I grab the picture I always keep on me. A lot of people here have wives and children waiting for them back home. Or parents eagerly waiting for their return.

The matted picture feels brittle in my grasp, but everything I want to see is still there. I think the photo was taken when I was seventeen and while my parents were out on a work trip. Gaya, Amy, Mathijs, and I snuck away to go paintballing. All of our hair is a complete mess, standing on all odds and ends. Out of the four of us, I have the least amount of paint on me, but there's a splatter of green going up the side of Mathijs's face, and a big red blob right in the center of Gaya's chest.

Mathijs has his arm wrapped around me, pointing the gun in the general direction of the camera, while Gaya is holding Amy bridal-style. Each one of us is smiling ear to ear like we have the whole world in front of us, and nothing could ever get us down. We're grinning like fools, even though the other team annihilated us.

It's what I imagined a happy family might look like. Whenever I come back from deployment, there's always a feeling like something's missing. Even though I live in my sister's spare room, it never feels like home. But out here? Sleeping in a random cot in the middle of fucking nowhere? With the chance of getting attacked while I'm asleep? This feels more like home to me.

We're all fish out of water here. All fighting for survival while having each other's backs. It gives us a sick sense of belonging and companionship. Like we're equals with the same goals.

"You gonna call the lover boy once you're back?"

I whip my head toward TJ and hold back a sneer. I don't like when people bring up Mathijs. I've thought of contacting him a million times. Check up on him beyond just looking on the internet. He isn't the type of person who carries hatred in his heart, but I don't think I could bring myself to look him in the eyes after practically vanishing off the face of the planet. But, *God*, do I miss him.

"Are you going to call Kendall back?"

TJ winces. "She told me she wanted to get married."

I snort. "God forbid a girl wants that."

"It was our third time seeing each other."

"And the third year you've been messaging each other. Get a grip." I roll my eyes and grin his way.

Since I enlisted, there hasn't been a day where I regretted my decision to leave home. That's a lie—there were a great *many* instances where I wished I was in the comfort of my own bed instead of practically killing myself during training drills.

If I stayed home, what would I be doing with my life? Catering to some man my parents chose? Pop out babies left, right, and center just to have something to fill my days? Maybe if I continued with my initial plan, I'd be a broke journalist getting shot at for entirely different reasons.

Out here, I can prove myself. Make a difference in a way I'd never have been able to back home. With every life that I couldn't save, there's one that I did. One person who can go home to wish their children goodnight one more time, or eat dinner with their family.

That type of reunion isn't waiting for me once I get back to America. But out here, faced with the prospect of debt, nothing becomes more priceless than embracing life.

I'm not out here for a noble purpose, but something far more selfish. My mother might not be proud of the person I've become. It doesn't matter what insults she throws my way, I know the impact I've made. I'm not here to defend my country, I'm here to protect people. What's my mother ever done but traumatized them instead?

I made my own family without her, and I'll do whatever I can to keep them safe.

CHAPTER 5

ZALAK

I always thought *a trip down memory lane* was an idiom that could never take physical form. But the Halenbeek manor hasn't changed one bit since I last saw it.

I can only half-appreciate the sight of the place when the skin around my eye is a swollen patchwork of black and blue. The mahogany beams are still warm against the gray stones of the manor. The fountains are blinding white. The hedges surrounding the property are cut to precision. The gardens Mathijs's mother used to spend her days in are bright with color—even the greenhouse is still bursting with life.

The only difference is the extra security and the number of animals. I almost ran over a chicken coming down the driveway, and a cat hissed at me when I parked inside the garage—another thing that's changed. It seems Mathijs developed a love for fast cars.

Tucking my helmet beneath my arm, I wipe my sweaty palms on my jeans as I glance at the cameras stationed all over the property. The guard at the gate told me I'd been set up at the pool house, even though I know for a fact that there are designated rooms for security on the main property.

The second he told me where I'd be staying, my muscles uncoiled. I couldn't think of anything worse than playing roommates with a bunch of random men again and intruding into Mathijs's direct space.

I scrunch my nose and wince from the movement as I round the main building and walk the long way to get to the pool house. That's a new smell. As I close in on the "security wing," I spot the next proof of change. A new barn has been erected against the side of the main house, leaving a faint smell of hay and manure in the crisp late afternoon air.

Climbing the few steps onto the porch, I help myself inside the pool house—actually, to call it that is a stretch. It's a sleep out within ten yards of the pool.

The few boxes of things I own are neatly tucked against one of the walls, next to the mini kitchen. This afternoon, some guy showed up at my doorstep and balked when he saw the state of my face. Apparently, Mathijs told me last night that he'd send a moving van over to get all my things. Honestly, that was news to me.

Numbness replaces the pain in my foot, lessening the amount

of strength I have as I subtly limp. It doesn't take long to peek into the bedroom and bathroom.

Returning to the main room, I hoist the first box up onto the dining table. It has all the food and drinks I own in it. Then I still when I open the fridge. The *fully stocked* fridge. I slam it shut and move to each and every cupboard. All filled to the brim with every food item I could possibly want.

I didn't agree to any of this.

I walk into the bathroom stocked with shampoos, conditioners, and soaps in the vanity. I fist the packet of hair accessories, and rummage through the drawers, eyeing all the sanitary products.

Was this all planned? Has he been patiently biding his time, waiting for me to hit rock bottom so he can swoop in and save me?

Well, fuck him. I don't need a goddamn hero. I've made it this far myself.

Storming to the bedroom, I whip open the wardrobe doors and—

Oh. Oh God.

Slowly, I reach for the blue jersey hanging on the rack. I run my fingers over the embroidery. Tears sting my eyes as the memory pushes up my throat to choke me. Gaya, Amy, Mathijs and I all have the same matching jersey from the time we snuck away to visit the Rocky Mountains together.

I never thought I'd see it again.

Placing it back on the rack, I grab the Ferrari leather jacket that Mathijs brought back for me after his trip to Monaco. Then the next item—my homecoming dress. Then a hoodie Gaya and I tried to bleach dye. Then the blouse I bought with Gaya during a family trip to Paris.

One right after another, memories slam into me as I sift through each article of clothing.

I never thought I'd see any of them again. Gaya told me that within a week of moving out, Mom got a maid to put all of my things into boxes to donate.

While I moved on with my life, he lived in the house owned by his dead parents, running his father's business, and holding on to my clothes. Ten years after I left him and everything I owned behind, they're back.

I squeeze my eyes shut, relishing in the ache. A sharp pain radiates through my foot, and I stagger back onto the bed. The softness of the duvet momentarily snaps me out of my misery. I forgot what expensive bedding feels like. From riches to rags and back to riches. It's not the circle of life I envisioned for myself.

I finish putting my meager belongings away, then meet with Sergei, the head of security, for a brief rundown of the compound. Once I'm back at the pool house, I slump down on the couch in front of the TV, holding a bag of frozen vegetables to my eyes.

Time ticks by, and the sun sets, changing the sky from orange to indigo. Despite the ache in my empty stomach, I can't bring myself to get up from the couch other than to refill my drink. Beyond a couple packets of ramen, the only food here belongs to Mathijs—and I won't accept his handouts.

I've done nothing to earn any of this. I shouldn't have agreed to move in early. I could've lasted two weeks in a tent until I started working somewhere.

Pushing myself onto my feet, I hesitate before deciding to track Sergei down. I'll ask him to pass a message to Mathijs: *Thank you, but I'll be on my way. See you in two weeks.*

Just as I reach for my shoes, a knock rattles the front door, jolting me into motion. Instinctively, I reach for the gun in the top drawer next to the door. Only when I flick off the safety and hold the weapon behind the door, out of sight, do I become mindful of my actions.

My heart stutters as I blink, transported away from a place where I could be attacked at any second.

What the fuck am I doing? There's no threat.

The silent alarms would be going off if there's anything wrong. Who the hell do I think is coming for me? The other security guards? The fucking maid? Jesus Christ, I need to get my shit together.

Tucking the gun into the waistband of my workout tights, I right my hoodie to cover the bulge. I look through the peephole then turn the handle, inching the door just wide enough for me to stick my head through.

Speak of the devil.

My chest aches at the sight of him. I've seen Mathijs in a suit countless times, but it's nothing compared to seeing him in one when he fills out the expensive fabric that shapes to his muscles.

His platinum hair is impeccably styled, and there isn't a single speck of dust on his jacket.

"Good evening, *Lieverd*."

He can't call me darling anymore.

"They said you'd be gone for the next week," I say.

Sergei was the perfect intermediary because Mathijs wouldn't have been there to convince me to stay. Now he's here to weaken my resolve.

His lips quirk to the side, showing me a hint of the boy I used to know. "Isn't it dangerous to have a set schedule?"

I narrow my eyes. "Is this a test?"

"No, but I can get someone to make you one." Paying no mind to my personal space, he forces me to back up as he leans against the doorframe and tucks his hands into the pockets of his slacks. The pose is casual, but it only makes me painfully aware of how much of a man he's become. "I remember how much you loved subtly dropping your good grades into conversation."

"People change." I bite the inside of my cheek, unsure how to navigate having a conversation, let alone how to process the spark of familiarity he brings.

"They do," he sighs. "But I fear there are certain areas of my personality that continue to pose as a plague to the people around me. There's no cure for it."

"Let me guess. You're still an obnoxious winner and a sore loser." I can't help but feel like I'm back in high school, hanging out with Mathijs when my biggest worries were my SATs and my overbearing parents.

"Ever the genius, Zal." His smile strikes me straight through the heart.

Zal.

TJ would always call me ZB. The last person to call me Zal was Gaya.

The single syllable wedges itself into my heart and threatens to tear me in two. I curl my fingers into a tight fist like it might fight off the memories of the people I've lost.

"Are you going to let me in, or would you prefer I help myself?" Mathijs wears a coy grin. If he's aware of my inner turmoil, he doesn't let on. Without waiting for my response, he grabs a brown paper bag off the floor and lets himself inside, ignoring my huff of protest.

His shoulder brushes mine as he passes, and a shudder goes down my spine as I remember all the times we've held each other. God, I forgot how much I've missed any kind of touch.

The bag crinkles as he sets it on the bench, then rummages through the cabinets pantry.

Crossing my arms, I glare at his profile and try to ignore the way he fills out his suit. The fabric stretches against his shoulders as he moves, and when he deposits his jacket on the bench, loosens his tie and rolls up his sleeve, it's like all semblance of decorum evaporates.

I'm transfixed on the ripple of his tendons and veins. It's screwing with my head.

Catching myself, I clear my throat. "What do you think

you're doing?"

"I'm safely assuming that you haven't eaten dinner, so I'm remedying the issue."

"Mathijs, stop."

He listens, complying only after pulling out the cutlery and tipping the *bakmi goreng* onto the plate.

"Mathijs," I growl.

He holds his hands up in surrender after stationing the container of soy sauce beside the plate.

"I can't accept this. Any of this," I say, exasperated, waving around the room.

"Be more specific, darling."

Prick. He knows exactly what I'm talking about.

"The pool house. The job. The food. *The clothes*." I point toward the bedroom. "All of it, Mathijs. It's too much and too far. I'll take my stuff, and I'll be back in two weeks and I'll move into the *actual* security wing like I'm supposed to. I can earn my way to a private residence." I run my hands through my hair, forgetting that I've braided it. "Thank you, but I can't take it, and I won't."

The silence stretches, thick and cloying, as he watches me with the intensity of a lion on the hunt. His eyes darkens as he peruses me. The light illuminates his sharp features, casting harsh lines beneath his jaw. I can hear the insects outside, the soft hum of the fridge, and the thunder of my heart.

Maybe he's disappointed in me. Maybe he's waiting for me to tell him to leave. Maybe—

"Did the military house you?"

"Yes."

"Feed you?"

I nod.

"Clothe you?"

"That's different," I argue.

"How?" He pushes off the bench and slowly makes his way toward me, one hand in his pocket. "You've been employed as my private security, and I think you are well aware that the extent of your job description isn't protecting me from pick-pockets, or holding my hand as I cross the street." Tilting his head, he purses his lips, looking like he's trying to navigate a minefield. "You might not know the full extent of the work my parents did, but I know that back in high school you were smart enough to figure out that my father was shot, and he didn't come home bloody because of a car accident."

I swallow. I was walking across the foyer just as his dad stumbled inside, clutching his shoulder and leaving a trail of blood on the floor. His mom yelled to call a doctor, and they looked at me with pity when I said he needed to go to the hospital.

The gunshot wasn't the first sign that Mathijs's family wasn't just into finance. Their guards always wore guns—the proper kind. Not a stun gun. There was security wherever they went, and bulletproof windows. Mathijs doesn't know this, but I saw crates of cash hidden in one of their ranches. Their vineyard had far more muscle than what was appropriate for that industry. The signs were all there.

Maybe I've bitten off more than I can chew by accepting this job. Who knows what kind of shit I'll be exposing myself to?

Really, I'm just making excuses. The prospect of danger has never stopped me from doing anything. I've been in war zones and full-blown shootouts more times than I can count. I've broken into heavily guarded places, played assassin, killed with my bare hands, and faced down men in underground fight clubs. Being muscle for a grinning mobster might be the least dangerous thing I've done.

The most difficult thing about this will be spending days around Mathijs without being sucked into a dark hole that I can't get out of. Because every time I'm with him, I'll be haunted by things I'll never be able to change.

I clear my throat and square my shoulders, hoping it'll instill some level of confidence in me. "Then what exactly am I doing for you?"

He shrugs. "Standard security work. Escort, lookout, raids."

"Raids?"

"Oh yes. They're a lot of fun. Gangsters, mafia, gunrunners. You name it."

"That's not the term I'd use."

I narrow my eyes as he circles me, his husky voice holding the slightest purr. "Darling, you've entered the land of mayhem. Surely you realized that when you accepted my offer."

"My head had been pounded into the concrete. I was potentially concussed. Bleeding from my forehead. Dehydrated. Stressed. And exhausted. I wouldn't call that clear, concise thinking. Raids are illegal." I cross my arms.

Leaning against the counter barely an arm's length away, copying my pose, he says, "Don't tell me you're a law-abiding citizen now. That would be rather boring."

"I made money from illegal fighting rings. I think my fear of the law is long gone." Really, the only thing I was scared of was my mother's wrath.

"Good. You were always too much of a good girl."

I cock a brow at him. It's hard to ignore the thrum of excitement in my veins. No more monotonous days. No more staring at a TV for countless hours, waiting for night to fall so I can go back to bed and attempt to sleep.

"I have arranged for a physiotherapist to come around tomorrow morning to help you with your nerve damage. She will be able to get you any medication and further treatment you might need."

My excitement comes to a screeching halt at the reminder that I've turned into his pity project. "You said I get medical insurance. I never agreed to physical therapy."

He gives me a knowing look. "Would you have gotten proper treatment to permanently fix it, or medicated just enough to function?"

Screw him for being right.

"Consider this a requirement of your employment."

Shaking my head, I say, "I can accept the job, the accommodation, and its perks. But the rest of it is too much. I don't know if you're doing this out of guilt or whatever it is you're planning." As if I need to prove something, I add, "I'm the one who fought and bled to get into Special Ops. I'm the one who killed to get those records."

Me.

Not my mother forcing me to do it. Not my father's—or any man's money. *I did it*. Mathijs helped get me into shooting and getting my hands dirty outdoors. But the rest was on me. I earned everything I have.

"Say what you like, but you're treating me like a charity case," I say.

The tension in the air is thick enough to slice through. Any semblance of playfulness is wiped completely off his face, replaced by a mask solely for business.

"If you don't want to accept what I'm offering out of genuine hospitality or kindness, then that's your prerogative. Not every deed is a business transaction. If you'd like, I can turn it into one so you can justify to yourself why you're allowed to accept it." Mathijs straightens and angles his body so we are perfectly parallel to each other. "So let me explain it another way: People want me dead. I need you sharp and functioning to ensure that doesn't happen. That means I need you fully recovered or on a quick road that way. I need someone who won't faint because they haven't eaten. I need someone whose head is clear because they aren't worried about making rent or when they can organize for an electrician to come in to fix the light. I need someone who can run when they get the order to run."

My body stiffens with each point he makes. They're all valid and completely faultless. Sleeping in a tent and waiting weeks to get an appointment with the doctor means that I can't do my job properly. And if I can't do my job, people die. And...

Fuck.

What was I even thinking? I can't do this job. My foot is screwed up. My brain is scrambled to shit. I can't bring myself to step foot inside a car. I have to stave off a panic attack every time I hear metal scrape against metal. Hell, my observation skills have become nearly nonexistent. How am I meant to protect him?

I shake my head. "If you want a soldier, that isn't me. I've been..." I search for the words that don't translate to *I've been rotting away for the past two years and I'm broken beyond repair.* "I've been off duty for two years, and my senses aren't as sharp."

"How many guards did you count between entering the gate and stepping inside this house?"

"Eight. Seven on duty. One coming off. Two gardeners and a maid."

"Of those eight, how many of them were women?"

"None."

"How many of them can blend into a crowd?"

"Zero."

"I have fifty-nine men on my roster. Over half of them have a military background—marines, special ops, rangers. All men. All with the subtlety of a neon sign. If anyone were to be taken out first, it'd be the men in suits. They're the first and only line of defense I'd have. Then there's you." His lips twist into a grin. "You could be on my arm, in a twenty-thousand-dollar dress, and no one would know that you could take them out in seconds. Beautiful. Violent. Deadly."

I don't deserve to be called beautiful. I most definitely haven't felt that way for years. Gaya, Amy, and I would go out whenever I was back, and we'd all get dolled up before dinner or hitting the town. But come morning, I was back to dressing like a woman my mother would never approve of.

These past two years I've been avoiding looking in the mirror because I don't want to see a ghost stare back at me—whether it's Gaya's, TJ's, or my own.

Mathijs inches closer until we're a foot apart, and I have to crane my neck to look up at him. There's too much reverence in his voice when he speaks. It curls around my stomach and makes me feel weaker than I've ever felt.

I want to lean in and place my head against his chest to absorb his warmth. I want to breathe in his scent, and believe his words, and feel less alone.

"I don't want a soldier. I want *you*. Anyone can pick up a gun. You? You don't need a weapon to become one." A soft smile curves his lips. "Although, I hear you're *exceptional* with one." He winks. "I take credit for it, of course."

My breath hitches when he tucks a strand of hair behind my ear. My eyes shut for the briefest moment, relishing in the slightest brush of his fingers against my skin. It sparks electricity through my veins and dies when it hits the shadows inside my soul.

The way he looks at me... like he's seen every part of me and

I really am exactly what he said. *Beautiful*. With my busted lip, swollen eyes, and broken soul.

"My little *Lieverd*." He appraises me with a beaming smile. "The best female sniper the world has ever seen."

His proximity makes me hyperaware of every inch of our skin and how easy it would be for him to touch me. I'm reminded that human touch can come without pain.

I shift my weight as I look over his shoulder. Anywhere but at him. "Not the best. She died a while back."

Mathijs's chuckle skitters down my spine and flushes my body with a warmth that I forgot existed. "So it's settled then. You'll stay," he says, backing away toward the exit.

Cockiness oozes from his pores as I glare at him. "I never—"

"The physio will stop by at ten a.m. Enjoy your dinner, Zal."

He shuts the door behind him before I get the chance to say another word.

Prick.

CHAPTER 6

MATHIJS

There are many ways to identify a counterfeit banknote.

The weight. The embedded security thread. Color. Paper texture. Ink. Watermarks.

This particular Franklin has all of those down pat, and more specifically, microprints. The small characters printed on banknotes that can only be seen beneath a magnifying glass.

I hold the note up to the fluorescent light.

Art. That's the only way to describe this masterpiece. It's beautiful. Truly.

The equipment needed to pull this off would have cost a fortune and several counts of armed robbery.

"I suggest you start singing, Mr. Ofsoski," I chime.

It's rather disappointing, needing to look away from the note to the buzzcut lumberjack-wannabe strapped to a chair in the middle of the soundproof room. Crimson beads along his full beard and drips down to his bare chest, and blotches of black and blue color his tattooed torso like watercolor. He's a subjectively bad piece of art.

I glance back at the note to get one last fill before placing it on the table, between the saw and mallet.

He throws his head to the side and spits on the shoes of my resident butcher, and the slightest *cling* against the leg of the desk makes me tip my head to the side.

A tooth. How lovely.

Here I was thinking we had pulled them all out already.

I sigh, clasping my hands in front of me, then pause right before I lean against the table. Internally rolling my eyes, I step closer toward the goon, changing my mind about soiling my clothes. Perhaps my cashmere coat wasn't the most ideal choice of clothing today. It'd be such a waste to taint it with the blood of a vermin.

One nod at Greg, and my butcher stalks forward to do whatever it is he's decided to do to Ofsoski. The asshole cries out, thrashing and cursing while Greg does something to his hands.

That reminds me, actually. I haven't thanked his wife, Linda, for the begonias she left for me last week. She's a delightful woman. I just don't trust her cooking. Nothing personal, but I don't have much confidence biting into minced meat when I know the Butcher. I'm not sure how the rest of my men can stomach going to his place for a barbeque.

I peer at the pliers in Greg's hand when he steps back. Oh, he took Ofsoski's nails. No wonder the man is slumped over like Satan's paid him a visit.

Sometimes nothing beats the basics.

I still remember the first time I liberated someone of their fingernails. There's a real technique involved when they have short nails. I, for one, don't particularly like it. The whole ordeal is far too messy.

"My patience is wearing thin." I check my watch and purse my lips at the time. We'll have to wrap this up if I want to make it home in time for dinner. "Tell me where you're producing the counterfeits, and I'll let you go."

"No," Ofsoski grunts, blood pouring from his gums.

"Now, now. No need to play hardball." I grin. "I just want to have a chat with your boss."

And take over Goldchild's business.

And make him regret not killing himself when he had the chance.

All those things are ironic since he's been trying to kill me and take over my business since my father killed one of his sons. Eye for an eye, and all that. Except I don't even know the name of his offspring.

For the past century, my family has taken care of the fake green that comes in and out of the state—a treasury, if you will. It's how we earned our place among the Exodus, the secret society I've lived and breathed since the second I was born.

Since my parents died, that job has fallen into my capable

hands. Well, the society would argue that I've been doing an absolutely horrific job at it since Goldchild has been a pain in my ass since the day I took over. The man is what would happen if a cockroach morphed with a leech.

I'd prefer if Goldchild moves shops and annoys the secret society in the East Coast instead. Or better yet, has a heart attack and takes his operation down with him—he'll leave his factory to me, of course. I wouldn't want such machinery to go to waste.

It'd put the Halenbeeks back in the Exodus's good graces. And I'd preferably like all of that to happen before the day of the Reckoning. It'd be rather unfortunate if I waste such a depraved night on politics.

"Fuck you. I ain't sayin' shit." He spits.

Again.

Men these days are disgusting.

"Surely you knew this was bound to happen eventually." I shoot his kneecap and he screams. "You and your merry band of idiots come to *my* territory." *Other kneecap*. More screaming. "Interfere with *my* business." *Left ankle*. "Kill *my* men." *Right*. "And you thought I would just let you do it?"

He wails. They always do. The sound is getting quite boring, honestly. Sometimes they have a higher cadence that tickles my eardrums unpleasantly. I prefer it when we can slap some duct tape over their mouths.

"All counterfeits are to be printed and approved by me, and any person wanting to try their hand at the craft asks for my permission, then gives me a cut. It's simple, really." I place my hand over my chest. "I like to think of myself as rather approachable. So you can imagine how offended I was when your boss decided to set up shop without consultation."

Ofsoski stares at me, breathing hard, hatred burning from each of his pores. The muscles are always harder to break.

"It seems my question is too difficult to answer. Then tell me this; does Goldchild have anything up his sleeves for our meeting tomorrow?" I give him an innocent smile. "I'll make your death quick," I promise.

Silence.

"Nothing?" I cock my brow. "Pity. I thought we were getting somewhere." Sighing, I fix my coat and leather gloves, then do a quick once-over making sure that there's no red on the gray material.

With a quick flick of my wrist, I grab my gun and fire a bullet into his shoulder. The resulting splatter—and ear-piercing cry—leaves a droplet of blood on the sleeve of my cashmere coat.

Even though he's probably in a little too much pain to pay attention to me, I point to my sleeve so he can see the damage he's done. "I just dry-cleaned this." I frown. "*And* it's a limited edition." Shaking my head, I turn to Greg. "Keep him alive for a week, would you?"

Greg grins. "Aye, sir."

I don't need to look at Ofsoski to know that he's paled ten shades. He's got an exciting seven days planned for him.

"Good man." I clap Greg on the shoulder.

A chorus of Ofsoski's grunts and cries follows me out the door as the Butcher has his way with him. I wouldn't normally prolong the inevitable, but I'm... irritated.

The word isn't nearly strong enough to describe how I feel about all my men who have died over the past twelve months. However, I have my own piece of art waiting for me at home. She's priceless and doesn't need anything more to be perfect. And I can have one night where everything around me isn't going to shit.

Bringing Zalak into this war isn't exactly ideal, but I'd be a liar if I said I'm not excited about the fact that *my* girl will be giving me her undivided attention for eight hours a day.

There was no way I could bring her into my fold without incentive, and I'm done waiting for the right moment to claim her. She needs a job, and I had an opening. Although, Robert—may he rest in peace—had the skill set of a toddler when it came to operating a sniper. Zalak makes for a phenomenal step up.

I check my watch, and the tension in my shoulders bleeds away ever so slightly knowing that I have ample time to get ready.

The ride home seems to take longer than necessary, and responding to emails is more tedious than usual. With every second that passes, my pulse beats harder against my skin. Excitement thrums through my veins, setting every cell on fire as I keep shifting in my seat and looking up from my phone to see if we're any closer. The last time I felt this way was when I was a kid waiting to see if Santa left me any presents.

I had moved out of our family home to go to college for a bit. I had every intention of forging my own way through the world and waiting until the mantel was passed to me. I thought I'd have at least another twenty years of freedom before the crown was placed on my head.

So I never had any intention of living in this house. I thought I'd live in my own house closer to the city and patiently waited until I made a name for myself.

Then Dad got badly injured and I moved back in to help Mom take care of him, and ease the workload off his back so he could rest. Then he died, and before I knew it, Mom's broken heart gave out from the stress. Then I was alone. No family. No friends. No Zalak.

Thursday night family dinners were gone. Sunday brunch with Mom stopped. It was just me, Sergei, and a big empty house.

I've done everything I possibly could to make the stone walls feel like a home again; I've added animals, doubled the number of plants inside, hired more staff and even let some of their children move in.

It doesn't matter what I do, or how much money I throw to give the ground life, nothing makes me want to go home. Halenbeek Manor is just an overpriced haunted house where I go to rest my head at night.

But that's changed.

The familiar feeling in my chest is what I have been yearning for since I lost my parents. It's been twelve days since I've been back, and I never thought I'd be so excited for my trip to end. So I can go home. To Zalak.

When the manor comes into view, a cold sweat works down my spine. The excitement turns to anxious anticipation. Everything has to be right.

I nod at the staff as I pass and ignore one of my advisors when he rings. The kitchen is empty when I reach it, and everything I might need is already laid out for me. I knew I shouldn't have told the head chef that I was planning on cooking. Even though she thinks my skills are slightly above average, she lays out all the ingredients and utensils like always.

This particular dish, however, I've perfected. I could make it with my eyes closed. I've been practicing for years, and when it comes to this, failure isn't in my dictionary.

An hour later, food is packed into plastic containers. Just like the last time I came to the pool house two weeks ago, I have to wipe my clammy hands on my pants as I make it up the first step.

My breathing feels harder than normal, and the cocktail of nerves and anticipation is making me heady. The lights from the TV flashes from behind the curtains. Ten years and she's back. *Finally*.

Since I was a kid, I've been dreaming about the day we would live together. Albeit this is entirely different from what I had imagined, but I'll take it. I'll do whatever is necessary as long as I can sleep knowing that she's within walking distance from me, safe, alive, and home.

I inhale deeply before knocking on the door, then step back, momentarily unsure about what to do or where to put my hands. Before I can decide whether to pull out my phone or nonchalantly stare into the distance, the door creaks open just enough to see half of Zalak's body.

Every time I see her, she disarms me. The word *breathtaking* was made for her.

Her hair is disheveled in her French braids, poking up from different angles. The look pairs appropriately with her worn T-shirt and sweats. Slight bruising still circles her eye and climbs up her jaw and forehead, but like every time I see her, I keep thinking that she could never be more stunning than she is in that moment. Whether she's in the middle of the ring, knocking some guy's lights out, or hobbling away with her loss, she's still otherworldly.

I just want to lean over and kiss her. I think that would fix every bad thing that's happened these last ten years.

"Mathijs." My name escapes her lips on a breath, the lips I've been yearning for since I was old enough to know what I want. "You're home."

Home.

I want to tell her that the main building isn't my home; it's wherever she's stationed herself. If she wants to be in the barn with the animals, I'll get my bag and we'll make it a permanent sleepover.

Zalak's face falls when she spots the takeout bag in my hand. "Mathijs..."

"Would you rather I throw it away?"

Her eyes widen like I've committed blasphemy of the worst degree, and it only makes my smile widen. It's the same trick I've been using to get Zalak to eat since we started dating in our teens. If there's one thing she hates, it's wasting food. It's probably the only good quality her mother had.

Huffing, Zal reluctantly holds her hands out, and my chest expands with triumph. I reach out to give the bag to her and snatch it back before she can get her hands on it.

"Do you mind if I join you for dinner?"

"Are you asking me if you can, or are you telling me that you will?" she asks flatly.

"Both will ultimately result in me joining you for dinner."

Choice is merely an illusion. Or at least that's the saying. With the power of delusion and misplaced confidence, I can get anything I want.

Anything except my parents, and, for the past ten years, the girl who ran away from me.

The Zalak from back then would roll her eyes or make a comment about my arrogance. Then she'd look away to hide her blush.

She used to smile all the time. She'd laugh, and my world would stop to hear the sound. She'd always direct her smile at me, and I'd remind myself that nothing else matters but her. Keeping that smile. Making her laugh. Helping her become the woman she'd be proud of.

And I lost all of that.

I spent years wondering if I did enough. Maybe it's my fault she didn't know I'd do anything for her. Maybe I didn't communicate it well enough. Maybe I should have tried harder to convince her to stay. Maybe I should never have left when she told me. Because now she's a specter clinging to her flesh, and I won't survive losing her a second time.

Wordlessly, she backs away from the door to let me inside. I leave my shoes on the rack next to the entrance, then help myself to her cupboards.

She's barely made a dent on the groceries I bought her, but I bite my tongue and keep the comment to myself. We've both done things to survive, and things to make us take comfort in meeting our graves.

Zalak switches on the light and the mini chandelier above the table illuminates the area. We navigate the kitchen to set up the circular dining table in the middle of the room. She pauses as soon as she sees me remove the *dal tadka* out of the bag, and I have to pretend like I didn't catch the pained expression across her face.

She isn't walking as stiffly as she usually does, and there isn't as much of a lean to the way she stands. Getting a physiotherapist to see her three times a week is clearly working.

And they say money can't buy everything.

I can feel her piercing glare on me as I plate up her food, piling on more than she could possibly eat, and it takes more effort than necessary to suppress my grin. What other choice do I have?

Zal grumbles something underneath her breath that sounds eerily similar to *fucking prick*, and I bite down my chuckle. I settle the plate in front of her and give myself a slightly larger proportion so she has no reason to complain or attempt to push her food to me.

"Thanks," she says, sounding less than grateful. Always so difficult, that one.

I pick up my naan and pretend not to watch her eat the *dal*. I think my heart stops beating as she chews, and I'm back to being a kid who's running home to show Mom the pasta necklace I made at school.

Zalak reveals nothing about her opinion on what used to be her favorite dish. When we were together, she was extremely vocal about her hatred for cooking. She loved *dal tadka* but her mother refused to make it because it was her brother's least favorite food. The one time I attempted to make it, we both decided it would be better to throw it out and stick to getting takeout.

I lick my lips and summon the courage to ask, "Do you like it?"

Her eyes snap up to mine like she forgot I was here, and I swear the corners of her lips twitch like she secretly wants to smile. "It's the best I've had in years. Where'd you get it?"

"I stopped by a place on the way here."

It's a struggle not to gloat or smile like I just got my first puppy. My heart doubles in size and I have to remind myself to eat as slow as humanly possible to stay in her company for

80

longer. But as the silence stretches, the same trepidation I felt on my walk here, slowly crawls back in.

I'm used to the silence. It's all I've known since my parents died six years ago. The only time I've had company over dinner was with business acquaintances or while being surrounded by strangers at a restaurant. This? It feels like we're strangers.

We used to know each other like the back of our hands, and sitting here, watching her eat like the mere act of it seems foreign to her, it feels like I'm back to knowing nothing but arm's-length relationships and hollow conversations.

I want to know everything there is about her. Is green her favorite color? Does she still like to play sad music while she showers? Is she still taking her coffee with milk, or has life made her take it black? Does she still want to get into journalism? Is she still a fire hazard who butters her bread before putting it in a toaster?

I take a sip of water to dislodge the discomfort in my throat. "Why did you choose to enlist?"

Zalak pauses, naan halfway to her mouth. My gaze drops to the scorpion tattoo on her hand, and I'm struck with the sudden urge to inspect it more closely. Slowly, she sets it down on the table and leans back in her chair, brows furrowed as if it's been so long she forgot what the answer is.

"After that... night—" She clears her throat and sits straighter in her chair, finally looking up at me. "There was nothing appealing about going to school to study journalism or politics or anything really." Her shoulders raise in a half-hearted shrug. "I had enough cash to get me by for a couple months, but then I had nothing left. I was struggling to get a full-time job, so I worked retail casually for a little while. Working in an office sounded like a nightmare. Then I saw an ad about enlisting. Food, shelter, pay, and a place that's completely unlike the life I grew up in—it was everything I needed at the time."

I try not to wince at that. She was constantly trying to prove herself to her mother, and it took me a while to realize that she ran away to prove her own worth to herself.

"And you chose to be a sniper? Why do I have a feeling shooting pegs at the vineyard inspired the career choice."

"Don't let it get to your head. You and I were only using farming rifles."

"Too late. I take full credit for introducing you to the world of guns." I smirk, then whistle as I lean back in my chair and appraise her. "From shooting bottles and washing pegs, to setting the record for getting a confirmed kill at thirteen hundred meters. The sky's the limit for you."

The red creeping into her cheeks only bolsters my confidence that I'll get my girl back. "The conditions were just right."

"Don't downplay your achievements."

She shakes her head. "I wouldn't have been able to pull it off if there were more of a breeze or a change in humidity."

"You set the record, Zal," I say softly.

"For women," she corrects. "There are men with double those stats. Allegedly."

Her answer makes me smile. Mainly because it means I can

start sprouting statistics and swoon her with random facts. "Women make up eighteen percent of the army, and only two percent of snipers are female."

Just as I thought, her eyes widen a fraction. I did my research and she knows it. The brownie points are in my bag tonight.

"The record holder for the greatest distance is a fifty-eight-year-old Ukrainian man. If you pull up a list of the top twenty longest recorded kills, not a single woman is on that list, and every man on there is either gray or their hairline has receded past the point of no return. In fact, you'd be on that list if that information became public. And you'd probably be the youngest."

Something heavy settles on my chest when she takes a staggering breath.

"Fifteen hundred meters."

I blink. "What?"

"That was my goal the second I specialized," she explains, pushing around the food on her plate. "A man in the 1800s has a confirmed kill from fourteen hundred meters. No scope, no spotter, nothing. Just an ordinary rifle. If he could do it, then so could I... at least that's what I told myself."

"You got close."

"Two hundred meters off isn't *close*." I grin at how defensive she gets, but I have to force it away when her voice makes a somber turn. "My mother died wanting another son. She finally got her wish."

"No, she got something better than that. A survivor."

83

My words hang in the air between us and I wish I could take them back so she would keep talking. So I can hear her voice and be reminded that all of this is real. I'm not dreaming of her return.

I can still remember the look she gave me before I thought I lost her for good. The sheer vehemence in her voice when she told me to leave. Why did I listen? Why didn't I insist on sticking around in case she needed me? I could have waited for her at the end of the driveway, or tried to sneak in through her window at midnight.

Maybe if I never left, both of our families would still be alive. Maybe she'd be a journalist, and Dad wouldn't have gotten sick, and Mom wouldn't have followed down the same path shortly after him.

I've been clinging to the hope that everything would go back to the way it was as soon as she returned. But that was a deluded wish that only naïve kids have. Still, I want to hold on to it because back then things weren't so empty.

I down my glass of water, then nod to the shirt she got on a school camp trip to the beach. "Remember when you got locked in the bathroom for two hours and you came back to the group bawling your eyes out?"

Zalak stiffens.

Fuck.

Fuck.

I can't think straight with her. Nothing I do is good enough when it comes to her. I should have settled for the silence. Hell, bringing up the weather would have been better than reminding her that I'm the lovesick puppy who has done nothing but wait around for her. I kept her clothes in my own damn room, for crying out loud.

When her eyes meet mine, it's an effort not to pull her into my arms. Because when she speaks, her voice breaks, and it feels like a hundred knives pierces my chest. "You kept my clothes."

"I did."

"For ten years."

"I would have held on to them for a lifetime."

Her eyes mist over. "You didn't know if I'd come back."

"I knew we'd reunite eventually. In this life or the next."

She doesn't respond to that. She doesn't do anything but help me wash the dishes and whisper thanks when she escorts me to the door.

Little by little, I'll get her back. Not the old Zalak, but the one who survived.

CHAPTER 7

ZALAK

I feel like a geriatric.

My neck hurts because I slept on it wrong. My back is aching because of an overly aggressive sneeze. To top it off, I have to wear sole inserts in my boot. If I thought gait training with the physio was demeaning, being told I have to wear the inserts as much as possible didn't sit well with my psyche.

Mathijs wasn't messing around with my rehab.

The physio comes over three times a week for an hour each time. I have a course of pain meds, and I'm expected to do the exercises three times a day as well. Honestly, my foot has never felt better. But I still haven't gotten nearly as much sleep as I should have.

The grass squelches beneath my boots as I head toward the

main house. Mathijs gave me a debrief of the full scope of my job description, the Exodus, and the current state of affairs within the counterfeit cash world. I don't know what the fuck I'm getting into, but at this point, I don't care.

After two and a half years, the monotony finally ends. I'm not spending my days looking forward to my next fight just so I can feel something. Now, every day will be slightly different.

Sure, I'll probably get sick of being a babysitter, but it's the only reason I've had to get out of bed.

A dollop of mud flies onto my cargo pants, and I groan as I pat it off. If I'm being completely transparent with myself, part of the nerves comes down to the fact that I haven't been this dressed up in years, and there's still the niggling feeling in my stomach that wants to impress him.

The late afternoon breeze sweeps through the air, and I shiver, zipping up the last few inches of my leather jacket. As per his highness's advice, I left the gun in a safe because I'm getting my very own untraceable weapon.

I pause when my phone vibrates in my pocket. Frowning, I read the text from Amy.

> **Amy:** I just got your recent payment. You really don't have to keep sending me money, Zal. It's been two years.

> **Me:** Gaya would have wanted me to take care of you.

Gaya wouldn't have wanted me to do a lot of the things I do

now. Sending Amy money is my way of making up for it.

Locking my phone, I continue toward the main house.

A group of men in suits and earpieces mill around the SUVs parked out front. I can feel their eyes on me as I climb the steps into the main house.

It looks homier than I remember. There's a lived-in feel about it that might convince a stranger that a whole family owns this house, not just one man. At least, it would appear domestic if there weren't so many armed men stationed all around the place.

Mathijs enters the foyer a second after I do. There's a subtle pinch between his brow, and an air of intimidation around him that I've never seen before.

Mathijs Halenbeek. Leader of the Halenbeek Empire. An Elder within the Exodus. This is the first time I've met this version of him, and I don't know what to make of it. But I can't help feeling some semblance of solace knowing that I'm not the only one whose skin had to turn into stone to make it through.

The one security guard stationed inside exits through the front door behind me. When the lock clicks shut, Mathijs's mask disappears. He drags his heated gaze from the top of my head down to the soles of my feet. A sly grin shapes his lips, and I'm like a deer caught in headlights. What on earth am I meant to do in this kind of situation?

I'm meant to be his employee, paid to keep him safe. Blatantly checking me out has to be in violation of every single code of ethics employers are meant to adopt.

"Come with me."

I square my shoulders. "Is that an order?"

"If that's what you prefer." He winks. "I recall you liked being told what to do."

Red flushes my cheeks in an instant. I gape at the space he once occupied and curse internally before scrambling after him. *Just like old times*.

That's an added stress I didn't think would come with the job—getting flustered because my ex-boyfriend-turned-boss hit on me.

And brought up our old sex life.

My first hour isn't getting off to a good start.

I clear my throat as I follow him into his office, which has barely changed. There's still a giant stag head mounted on the wall, with two smaller ones on either side of it. He's still using the same antique, green rug, and leather couch, and the grand table facing the middle of the room.

He stations himself by the long meeting table where a pool table once stood. Maps and various ledgers and stacks of cash are strewn across it, haphazard yet organized. I still once more when he rakes his gaze up and down my body.

I bite the inside of my cheek. "Sorry, I wasn't given a uniform." Was I meant to ask for one, or did I wrongly assume that it would just be handed to me?

"Good. Because you don't have one."

Right. I'm meant to blend in... I look at my combat boots, cargo pants, and leather bomber jacket. I most definitely do not fit in. I look like I've stepped straight out of a post apocalyptic video game.

"You've dressed beautifully." His lips quirk into a childish grin as my skin burns under the weight of his compliment. "Although, you would look better without all of it."

Lord, help me.

High school pickup lines.

I cross my arms, suddenly feeling like I'm seventeen years old, listening to every single horrific pickup line he managed to find online. "You're going to get a sexual harassment lawsuit if you keep this up."

"That's why you're a contractor. Can't sue me then." He taps his temple, signaling that he thought it through. "It would be unfortunate for my hired guns to unionize. The Halenbeek Enterprise HR team has enough on their plate as is."

I roll my eyes, and for some reason, his smile turns beaming. The sight makes my chest squeeze. Mathijs has started wearing my defenses down far too quickly and it's unsettling me. I'm not sure whether I'm turning into a stranger or into someone I've always known.

Before I can overthink the heavy shift in the air, he launches into explaining today's excursion. "I've arranged to meet with an informant who has intel regarding Goldchild's shop." He points to a spot on the map. "It's an abandoned factory out west in a commercial area. One of my men has scouted it and identified three possible locations for you to set up." He taps three spots surrounding the factory. "You'll be the eyes of this operation. If this is a setup, shoot to kill."

My lips part, not because of what's being asked of me, but because *he's* the one telling me to pull the trigger. It's hard to reconcile the fact that this is the same man who made pillow forts with me and memorized the recipe for microwave mug-brownies.

I swallow and nod. I admit, I'm looking forward to having a rifle back in my hands.

"The society I'm part of, the Exodus, has been up my ass. They wanted Goldchild's head on a platter last week. I don't care what needs to be done, I want him on a pike Vlad the Impaler–style."

Right. Best I can do is shoot him.

I nod once more.

Sergei joins us a moment later to debrief me on the plans, including times, streets, and best- and worst-case scenarios. My head swims with information, but the familiarity of it all has my blood thrumming. It's a heady mix of excitement and the anxiety of imminent death.

When the door shuts behind Sergei, I revert my attention to Mathijs, waiting for an order or some indication that we're going to head out—or more specifically, *I'm* allowed to head out to scout the area first.

Unless... Am I meant to be playing personal bodyguard *then* get myself up on a roof? "Uh, am I riding with you?"

His eyes brighten. "Take out the *with* and it's an enthusiastic yes."

"What?"

"Nothing."

Right.

I frown.

Mathijs reaches beneath the desk and throws a backpack toward me. I catch it midair. "What's this?"

"Open it."

He smirks all mischievously, and I narrow my eyes at him. Cautiously, I unzip the unassuming backpack and pull out the hard shell casing within.

"Code is four-nine-seven-two-six."

I spin the dials and the latch clicks open. My eyes drift to him once more before I swallow whatever skepticism I have and open the lid, then unpack the contents.

My shoulders fall. God, I'm dramatic. I was a specialist sniper. I've been hired to be his sharpshooter. Of course he's giving me a fucking rifle. *Duh.*

Even disassembled, the cool metal is a comforting presence in my hand. Like muscle memory, I spring into action, putting together the sniper like there's someone holding up a timer and yelling at me to hustle.

I internally smile when the last part clicks into place.

I still got it.

Flipping the weapon over, I point it to the floor to inspect every detail of it, only to still at the serial number at the bottom. My lips part. "This is property of the US military."

He shrugs, looking far too smug for his own good. "Perhaps."

"How did you get this?"

"I'm resourceful."

"It's illegal for you to have this."

"Darling, everything I do is illegal." He winks. "You'll find that it's more fun that way."

Shaking my head, I disassemble the weapon and return it to its case. Honestly, I expected nothing less. For some reason, I thought he'd be buying off gunrunners who do it all *off the books*. There's poetic justice in pulling the finger at the government while using their guns to circulate counterfeits.

"There's more."

I pause just as I'm about to return the case into the bag. Sending him a questioning look, I inch the front zipper open. *This motherfucker*. I wave the Cheetos in the air and raise a questioning brow.

He grins like this is his best work. "In case you get hungry."

The Capri Sun wobbles in my hand.

"It's important that my staff stays hydrated."

Fucking hell.

"You're impossible."

"I'm a good employer."

"Should I ask what Sergei has in his pack?"

"Zalak, you should know better than to ask what's in a man's bag."

I scoff, packing everything back up. "Nothing particularly useful, usually."

He chuckles. "It makes us feel important to have one."

"When was the last time you wore a backpack?"

"I don't need to *feel* important, when I already am it."

I shake my head and shoulder the bag, leaving the room without getting dismissed first. In the military, I would get my ass kicked to Sunday and back if I did that. Here? What's he going to do? Fire me? Somehow, I doubt that.

I run through a checklist of everything I need to do once I reach the meetup spot. Anxiety prickles up my spine, but for once, it's the good type of nerves. Without fear, people who go into war zones don't come out.

There's a line of SUVs parked right in front of the house. One of the doors is open for Mathijs and—

Every cell in my body goes cold.

I didn't think this through. Why the fuck didn't I remember that these kinds of jobs involve *that*?

Sweat gathers down my spine and my heart rate triples its speed. I whip my head around like we're seconds away from blowing up into a hundred parts. I haven't been inside a car in over two years. Buses are fine. Trains are doable. A car? Especially a fucking SUV?

No.

No.

I can do it.

I'm not there anymore. TJ—

No. I have to focus. I need this job. I can't afford to lose it.

Pain flares in my foot and the sound of scraping metal rings through my ears as I force myself to take a step forward. Images of TJ's body flash before me. The fire. The shards of metal. The screaming. Gunshots.

I can't do it.

I can't—

"Zalak."

I grab a fistful of the person's clothes, ready to slam them onto the ground and pummel their head in.

"Zalak," Mathijs whispers, a soft smile curving his lips like he's oblivious to my state. The creases of concern around his eyes are a dead giveaway. He motions to the side of the house, making no move to get my hand off him as my lungs burn with my rapid breaths. "Your beast awaits."

I follow the direction he's pointing to—a sleek black motorcycle. He... he knows. Swallowing, I quickly extract my fingers and mutter a quick thanks. Fuck, I need to get my shit together. I can't lose it on my first goddamn day. I'm here to do a job and prove I'm wholly competent for it. So far, I've proven that I'm anything but.

If I had this kind of reaction in the military, I would be suspended faster than I could line up a shot. Balling my fists, I focus on my surroundings—tallying up the guards, the exits, the clear skies, the lack of movement in the bushes.

I'm not there anymore. I repeat that mantra until I'm sick of it.

Safe isn't a word I can use today. My foot seems to develop a sixth sense for incoming danger, because the pain alleviates with each step. Avoiding eye contact becomes a no-brainer once I have my helmet firmly in place, and I can pretend to know what I'm doing. Fake it until you make it.

Except in this case, faking it could mean someone dies. No pressure.

The motorbike rumbles to life beneath me, and I rev the engine before taking off toward the meeting point. The gates open before I even reach them, then I'm on the road. The exhilaration of zipping down the road can't be replicated inside of a car. Nothing compares to the freedom of being outside a metal can.

I navigate onto the highway and off into the industrial area. As expected, it's near deserted this late in the afternoon. No one in their right mind would be working at this time on a Sunday. There's a slight chill in the air that sets me on edge. Everything is stiller, like the forest has quietened right before an oncoming attack.

Parking two blocks away from the spot, I slip my earpiece in and scout the area, taking inventory of every building, every movement, every conceivable thing that could pose a threat. Cars still drive past on the main road. I saw a homeless man pushing a trolley in the opposite direction, three blocks away.

There's the occasional chatter coming from the device about their ETA. Otherwise, I tune it out because I reach the place where the meetup is going to happen. Five tall buildings circle the spot. It's a sniper's worst fucking nightmare.

Who the fuck chose to meet here? Five multistory buildings. *Five*. One looks like it might be an empty office building. One's an abandoned factory, another is a car garage, and there are two big-ass sheds.

Too many blind spots.

I'm going to argue with Mathijs if he suggests meeting *anyone* here again.

If Sergei chose it, then he's lost my respect.

I can't protect Mathijs from shit at a place like this.

Grumbling beneath my breath, I pick the abandoned factory. It's the tallest and the least likely to have any workers inside. There's also a fire escape for me to speed down if there's an emergency. Out of all the buildings, I figure that the sheds are the lesser threat when it comes to hidden snipers. And I can't shoot at someone in the office building if I'm inside.

The rusted ladder creaks under my weight despite how hard I try to stay quiet. It has to be at least four stories high, and if the lack of dust on these handles are any indication, I'm not the only one who thinks this is a good place to set up for the view.

Empty beer bottles and broken glass litter the roof. I sidestep a bong and avoid the two needles to situate myself at the corner. It's a shit spot, but at least I'll have a clear view of the chosen meeting point, and a partially obstructed view of both ends of the street.

A helicopter passes in the distance, and I flinch. Momentarily thrown back to a place where sand crunches beneath my boots, and the blistering heat tears at my skin.

Clearing my head, I remove the backpack to assemble the rifle. The motion of getting ready for potential battle fills the hollow part of my soul. *This*, I know how to do. Clean a gun, put it together, shoot. I'm good at these things, and *fuck* if it doesn't feel good to have a sniper in my hands again. As fucked up as it is, I'm hoping I get to pull the trigger.

I grab the binoculars and spend a couple minutes scanning the area, paying extra caution to the office building. None of the roofs or windows seem to have any snipers, but again, what do I fucking know? From this position, I won't find out until they shoot.

Each movement catches my attention. Every sound makes me still. The four birds to the left perched along a windowsill, the candy wrapper floating along the street, the lone pigeon that sings every forty seconds.

If I had it my way, we would relocate or meet at a different time. But this is just how it's going to be. And if Mathijs dies because he chose a shitty location, I'm going to kill him.

"All clear to enter," I report to Sergei. Mathijs is ninety seconds out and two minutes late for the meet. "Green isn't here," I say Goldchild's code name.

"Moving in."

I don't recognize whose voice that is, which isn't surprising.

I settle onto the floor, attempting to get comfortable even though my knees are digging into the concrete. Supporting the rifle on the ledge and my shoulders, I peer down the lens and do another sweep of the area. Another downside to my spot is that there's no way for me to conceal my position. On the other hand, all I need to do is drop down and I'm sheltered behind the cement walls. You win some, you lose some.

It feels wrong to do this without TJ. It feels wrong to do

this alone in general, but *especially* without him. He had more experience than me, which made him the perfect spotter. The lack of shit talking makes this whole situation seem foreign. I say a silent prayer that his crazy ass is up there getting drunk and watching over me.

The thrum of engines grows louder with our team's approach. They park opposite my chosen building and leave the three SUVs running.

Mathijs being Mathijs chooses that moment to break security protocol and step out of the vehicle to conduct his search of the surroundings. Most of the guards join him in surveying the area.

His head is perfectly centered down my scope. I could have made this shot when I was sixteen. What the fuck is everyone thinking? How the hell has he survived this long if he's apparently got so many enemies.

"Return Edelhert to the vehicle." Annoyance slips into my voice. No one has died under my protection, and I don't intend to change that now.

The corners of every sniper's dream target's lips tip up like he's heard me. He searches the buildings until his green eyes penetrate through the lens and has me momentarily disarmed. Age has done that man wonders. Mathijs winks just as one of the guards whispers in his ear—I assume it's to politely tell him to get his ass into the car with the tinted, bulletproof windows.

Surprisingly, he complies. I don't breathe any easier once he's out of the kill zone, but being behind a rifle gives me a sick sense of calm. It's like having my body evolve in a matter of seconds.

Sights become clearer, sounds become louder, the breeze feels like a gust of wind. In this space, there's nothing but me and the other end of the gun. Everything else ceases to exist.

This whole thing would be better if I had someone beside me. I've never been on watch without a spotter before. There's no one to watch my six in case someone creeps up on me, or if there's commotion where I can't see. It doesn't help that I have no idea how trained Mathijs's guys are either.

Fuck.

I should have talked this through before we left. No one I've come across has struck me as shady, but it's hard to tell. There are always scorpions hidden in the sand—literally. It's the whole reason I got my name. I sat to readjust my boot while we were in the Middle East, and I almost died from one.

Tightening my hold around the rifle, I keep sweeping the area, going back to the SUV every few seconds to make sure he hasn't moved position.

"Vehicle approaching south from Wilson Ave," a voice comes through my earpiece.

I angle the gun in that direction and spot a single sedan heading our way. The men collectively stand taller and grip their weapons tighter.

"Weapons hot," Sergei says.

The car's plates have been conveniently removed, and it's fully tinted so I can't make out how many people are waiting in the car. It doesn't smell like an ambush, but it takes one person to make a kill shot. Something feels off. If what they're saying about Goldchild is true, he wouldn't come here in a single car. There would be some level of muscle that would rival Mathijs's.

"Give me reports." Sergei's voice sounds through my earpiece.

"I have eyes on a black sedan," I say.

"North end is clear."

"Western alley is clear."

"East's all clear."

"Nothing suspicious on the main road."

Something's wrong.

Goldchild pulls up across from Mathijs's car. It isn't until someone steps out that one of our men opens the door for Mathijs.

Idiots. They're meant to wait for an all clear first.

The barrel of my gun is trained on the newcomer, perfectly centered for a clean shot. I don't recognize him from any of the pictures of known members that I was given last night. Hired muscle maybe? Or a random man from their organization?

A plain brown envelope sits in his hand, too thin to pose any kind of threat unless there's a razor hidden in there. Or poison.

Wordlessly, he passes the envelope to one of our men before returning to his car to drive away. It isn't until they're revving down the street that the item is passed to Mathijs. Slowly, he opens it with his gloved hands, then unfolds the single sheet of paper.

He holds the letter up for me to see, and there, in black marker are three words:

FUCK YOU, CUNT.

CHAPTER 8

ZALAK

Mathijs leaves the compound nearly every day. I usually drive to the location first to scout it, set up on a roof or behind a window. Or sometimes I'm a couple meters away from him, pretending to be a random civilian who's enjoying a meal, not someone armed and ready to kill. Cafes, restaurants, bars, clubs, I've been everywhere with him over the last three weeks.

The days aren't monotonous, but there's a level of consistency that gives me enough semblance of normalcy, which doesn't make me feel like I'm losing control. Shit, I haven't once thought about sneaking away to have a go in the ring for some extra cash. I actually like what I'm doing.

The other day, I pretended to be his date at a yacht party. It would have been a little demoralizing to be his mindless arm candy if it weren't for the fact that we kept our hands to ourselves except for the occasional touch on my lower back as he steered me through the crowd. I think he realized partway through that I made for a horrific date because I wasn't going doe-eyed and melting for him. The touches were nice, but it made me spiral, questioning whether it's too much or too far.

Now, after a week on the road, it's good to be back on the compound. I've missed being able to anticipate my surroundings.

I tap my finger on my arm and try not to fidget as I wait for Mathijs to come out of his office. We were meant to leave for an undisclosed location twenty minutes ago, and the anticipation is agonizing. Sergei had absolutely no idea where we were meant to go since there were no outings planned, which only made him alert—and dare I say it, *upset*—that we were heading out, and the big man never gave him the heads-up.

"Apologies for my tardiness," Mathijs says before he exits his office. "Now, shall we?"

My lips part as I take him in. What in the fuck is he wearing? He looks like he's walked right off a military catalog with the black camo pants, combat boots, and military jacket. Mathijs is dressed to the nines, ready for war, and not a single one of his security detail has a goddamn clue what we're about to walk into.

No wonder Sergei has lost all his hair working for him.

"Where, pray tell, are we going?" Jesus Christ. Is that a tactical knife strapped to his leg?

He rubs his hands, eyes glinting in excitement. "On an adventure."

My hair is graying with each second. "You're a security nightmare," I mumble, following behind him down the steps.

"I know," he throws over his shoulder.

We turn toward the ammunition room and I have to stop myself from outwardly groaning. If he's planning another raid or mission, he's meant to involve *his fucking security advisors*. There's absolutely no way I am about to agree to go off on some *adventure* when I'm the only one who can protect him. It's plain stupid, especially with Goldchild growing more aggressive with each passing week.

The combination of annoyance and anticipation has me crossing my arms and staring him down as he unlocks the hidden entrance, and the bookshelf automatically slides back into the wall and to the side. "Tell me where we are going, so I can advise Sergei to prepare accordingly."

He waves his hand dismissively. "No need. All the necessary arrangements are done." I catch the sniper rifle he throws my way and glare at him. "It's just you and me today, *Lieverd*."

"I'm calling Sergei."

"You're no fun." Mathijs sighs, grabbing a fire-resistant blanket and a spotting scope, placing both in a pack that he throws over his back. I glare at him when he grabs both my shoulders and taps my nose. "Don't worry, my little protector. We're staying on the property."

Mathijs snatches the rifle from me before I get the chance to respond.

I repeat, what the actual fuck is going on?

Dumbfounded, I march behind him into the forest surrounding his property, no closer to figuring out what shit show I'm about to find myself in. "Give me that." I try to snatch the sniper from him but he tightens his grip. So I hold my hand out instead. "I'm meant to be protecting you. Not the other way around."

He whirls around on me. "You're unarmed?"

"The answer depends on who's asking. Are you expecting a show and tell?"

"Are you offering? Maybe throw in a pat down as well." Mathijs's eyes glint. Flirting with the flirt will only make this whole situation even more difficult to navigate.

He grins victoriously, and I resort to following along silently. The dirt squelches beneath my feet, and my pants catch on branches and bushes. The Halenbeek estate consists of acres of forestry spanning over ten miles. The first time Sergei told me, I was ready to argue about how horrific an idea it was. Now that I'm walking past trees and rocks and fallen logs, I can just spot the various hidden cameras and pressure systems concealed beneath leaves. Apparently, an alert will go straight to the security room if there's anything bigger than a cat passing by.

My foot aches as we walk, but it's nowhere near as bad as it used to be. Since I started, Mathijs always makes sure that there are no scheduled outings when I'm meant to have a physio appointment. And the times we've gone out of the city, he forced me to "see her" by video.

Mathijs halts in his steps, stopping us at the edge of a clearing of green fields and a small lake that continues in a stream straight ahead. I frown when he draws a set of binoculars out of his bag to peruse the area. Are we... hunting? When we were kids, he wouldn't hurt a fly but he wouldn't think twice about laying it on someone else.

Ex-wannabe-veterinarian-Mathijs doesn't hurt animals. Or at least I thought that was the case until he sets the binoculars down and lays out the blanket on the ground, right behind a log.

"What are we doing out here, Mathijs?" I say wearily. I can shoot humans fine; animals are where I draw the line.

"Target practice."

Excuse me? "For... you?"

"It wounds me you think I'm the one who needs it." He places his hand over his heart, then drops onto his knees on the blanket.

"Are you saying I'm not a good shot?"

"I'd say no such thing." He settles himself on his stomach and places the rifle in front of him, balancing it on the log. I try to spot what it is he's aiming for, but all I can see on the other side of the clearing are more trees.

Averting his attention, he reaches into his backpack to hand me the scope. Fucking hell, I guess we're doing this. I kneel beside him and take the spotting scope from him.

"I hope my instructions weren't confused for miles."

What?

He squints somewhere north, and I follow his line of vision until I spot a human-shaped dummy with target symbols all over it.

"Fifteen hundred meters, right? That's the distance you want to meet."

I stare at his profile for a heavy moment.

He... he's helping me try to reach my goal? My chest warms and expands, faster than I can reasonably comprehend. Putting a roof over my head and giving me a salary felt like an act of community service. This is another layer altogether.

My head swims with all the things I could say: thanking him, rejecting his offer, insisting that he doesn't need to waste time accompanying me. But anything I want to say is caught in my throat.

"I think I need glasses," he mutters as he squints in the direction of the dummy.

I swallow and force myself to look away. I just know that my body is humming with the familiar thrill of... of working toward something.

I forgot what that feels like. *Goals.*

Shit. Ambition is such a mundane, everyday concept, but already it's made me feel ten times lighter.

Bringing the scope to my eye, I take a deep breath and play around with the dials to work out the distance to the target. "We need to go closer. We're about eighteen hundred meters."

He curses under his breath. "Let's hope you never find out what your observations do to me."

"What?"

He smirks. "Nothing you need to worry your pretty little head about."

I hit his arm as we rise to our feet.

"I cannot believe you just attacked your employer." Mathijs mock-gasps.

"Sue me then," I deadpan.

Chuckling, he grabs the bag, while I carry the blanket. "Many fathers teach their children essential survival skills. Like how to light a fire, check the car oil, and fish. Mine taught me to always have my lawyer on speed dial."

"I look forward to hearing from them." I roll my eyes and walk closer to the middle of the clearing. "Make sure you mention that I am interested in perfecting a fifteen-hundred-meter kill shot—and I already succeeded at thirteen. Live targets are always welcome."

"You murderous little thing. I like it."

I side-eye him, but the corners of my lips curl at the deranged compliment. Using the scope, I get us as close to the fifteen-hundred-meter point as I can and lay out the blanket.

Mathijs offers me the rifle, but I motion for him to get into position. "Let's see how good your aim is."

"No need." He holds out the rifle again. "Just trust me when I say it's phenomenal."

I push the weapon back to his chest, preparing to say the

magical words that could get this man to do anything. "I bet you can't make the shot."

His eyes harden, and he's on the ground with the gun poised within the next breath. Simply put, his form is horrific. Not to mention he's balancing the rifle on his shoulder when there's already a stand attached to it for him to use.

"You already have support. Use what you have around you. There's no point reinventing the wheel." He readjusts, pulling his knee too high up to the side, jeopardizing the stability and straightness of his body. "No, you're too angled. Square your shoulders. Don't put your elbows there."

"Anyone ever told you that you're such an eloquent teacher?"

"You're the one who taught me how to shoot," I say, then grate out, "*Form*," when he reverts back to the position I just got him out of.

"The teacher becomes the master. A classic." He shakes his head, then readjusts his hands on the gun.

I glance at Mathijs as small smile curls across my lips. This is the happiest I've felt in years, and it's all because of him. There's no serious conversation about our pasts or how we see the future shaping. This is just Mathijs and Zalak, hanging around in the forest and playing with guns just like we did when we were teenagers. Right now, we're two friends with nothing but this moment.

Part of me wants to lean over and throw my arm over his waist and snuggle into his side like we used to. But we can't do any of that because everything has changed. He's my boss now. Even if he weren't, I have far too much baggage, it'd be cruel to force anyone to share the load with me.

Lowering myself onto my stomach beside him, I fix my attention on Mathijs, and say in an even tone, "Take a deep breath, then look down the gun."

He does exactly as I say, body tense. Oh, such a rookie.

There's a certain elegance that comes with using a sniper that can't be replicated in any other form. The level of patience required to carry out an intel-gathering mission would have most people clawing their eyes out. But there's peace in studying others. You start gathering details about your environment that you wouldn't have seen before. Like the fallen bird's nest a hundred meters south. Or the deer half a klick behind us, and the blue jay we passed on the short walk between our last sniper's hide and here.

"Usually, your spotter will help you identify your target and the conditions that would impact the shot," I explain as I bring the scope up to my eyes to focus on the dummy hidden among the trees. I commend whoever set up the target for not putting it in a wide-open space.

"You just aim and shoot."

"Amateur," I tease. I had that exact thought before I started training. I said it to TJ once as a joke, and he almost hit me over the head for it. So I told him that he was just jealous I was a better shot. "A bullet doesn't fly through the air; it falls in a specific direction. For a shot at this distance, you need to consider the Coriolis effect."

I hear Mathijs move beside me—to give me a blank stare, I assume. "I believe that piece of knowledge is above my pay grade."

"It's the pattern of deflection taken by objects not firmly connected to the ground that are moving a long distance."

"That's even further away from my pay grade. But keep going, seeing you nerd out turns me on."

I drop the spotting scope and hiss, "*Mathijs.*" I point at his shoulders. "Focus—and watch your form."

"I'll be honest, I can barely line up the target," he says nonchalantly before resuming his position. "I swear it's moving, and you getting all smart and bossy is doing things to me."

"Aim for something closer then," I suggest, moving around to find something else for him to shoot. "How about the—"

A shot rings out, and my first instinct is to drag him behind me, but I stop when he says, "Sorry. I got bored." He rolls to the side and hands me the sniper. "I believe I'm better suited to an observer role."

"What did you hit?"

"Nothing alive, one would hope." He shuts his eyes like he's concentrating. When he reopens them, there's a disappointed look on his face. "Fortunately, I don't hear any screaming, which means I am still on track to winning boss of the year—you, on the other hand, do not have any Christmas bonuses on your horizon."

"Give me four working days to cry about it." We swap gadgets. I set up the sniper by fixing the height of the stand and leveraging the ground to my advantage to stabilize the kickback.

"Make that two—I'm on a tight deadline."

I shake my head and take a deep breath, saying a silent prayer up to TJ and Gaya before looking down the scope, making all the necessary adjustments to see the dummy better.

"You make it look so easy," Mathijs says after a moment of silence.

Scoffing quietly, I say, "I haven't pulled the trigger yet." It's been a long time since I've tried aiming at anything more than eight-hundred meters away, and I've almost forgotten how difficult it is. "I have to calculate the bullet drop due to gravity, spin drift, wind, light, elevation, barometric pressure, and the final kinetic energy upon arrival," I explain.

"Who would have guessed AP physics would come in handy."

I huff out a half-hearted chuckle, calculating the range to the target and the estimated descent, but the world is working against me regardless of how much compensation I try to make for the angle and the amount of light on the target.

"Approximately forty-five-degree winds coming from the southwest. There's an incline. Plus, the humidity is too high, so the impact will be lower."

"So what does that all mean?"

I pull the trigger between heartbeats, then narrow my eyes at the target.

"It means I'll miss the shot."

CHAPTER 9

MATHIJS

G oldchild sent me a gift.

Another one of my men. Dead.

A severed fucking head in a pretty white box wrapped in a blue bow.

"Where did you find it?" I growl, staring at the bloody and blue face.

The kid's only twenty years old. I recruited Tommy myself. All he had to do was move nonvaluable stock from one place to another. He had a sick sister he wanted to take care of, and I was covering her treatment.

"The box appeared this afternoon at the West Point warehouse," Sergei says with a scowl. "We've got nothing on who dropped it or what time. The footage was wiped."

Goldchild has been getting bolder by the day, and the Exodus has been giving me hell for losing control over the situation. All they care about is that we're bleeding money. They don't give two shits about the fact that my men are getting slaughtered like fucking animals.

I curse, swiping a hand over my face.

How many more innocent people need to die for this ridiculous feud? I don't even know why my father killed Goldchild's son, or when. Sergei hasn't been able to color in the blanks either.

"Have you told his sister?" I ask.

He shakes his head.

I exhale slowly, trying to come up with a plan. "We're going to continue to cover her treatment, and send her whatever amount Tommy was receiving, plus twenty percent. I want eyes on her at all times for the next two months in case that fucker tries anything."

"And the warehouse?"

"Comb it. I want forensics in, and for you to personally question each and every man and woman who's been through there in the past twenty-four hours. Reach out to all our informants to see if anyone has any information on who carried out the kill and where the rest of his fucking body is."

A good person died for green and vengeance. Tommy's never even picked up a gun, or done anything worse than committing traffic offenses. Goldchild's gone too far this time.

"Tell everyone that Tommy is going to be buried at the end

115

of this week, so his entire fucking body better be in that coffin."

"Yes, sir."

This is all a fucking mess.

I've put in a request to the Exodus to spare more men and resources so I can end this nightmare, but all they've done is sit on their hands. We're meant to be above the government and everything else the sun touches, and yet they're leaving me to clean up the mess I have no doubt they all had a hand in.

My father died long before he could prepare me to deal with more than just psychological warfare. I feel out of my depth with all of this.

"Is there anything else you suggest?" I ask. Sergei was my father's right-hand man. There's no way I would have survived this long without his help. The men respect him, and he knows how to survive this world. It's more than I can confidently say about myself.

"Send a message."

My eyes snap up to his. "Spilling more blood will only make it worse. Their retaliation will hit harder."

"They killed one of your men," he says solemnly. "Goldchild needs to know what happens when they act in cold blood."

I frown, thinking about it for a moment. We've been on the defensive for too long. We've always acted out of necessity and in proportion to Goldchild's crimes, staying above the dirt he's been throwing our way.

"You're right. Get it done."

I massage my temples and stare at the mountain of paperwork on my desk. Some days, I'm not sure whether I prefer the legal or the illegal side of my family's business. No one is dying in the hedge fund world, but I might drown beneath all the paper.

Tommy's severed head flashes through my mind. I've been working for over fourteen hours. I need a break. Luckily, I have the perfect cure to a bad day.

Pushing out of my chair, I jog out of my office and into my backyard, following the winding path toward the pool house.

Perhaps I have become a psychic of sorts. Or perhaps I am wise beyond my years. Because there she is, sitting on the little porch, staring at the night sky.

Call it intuition that she'd be out here. A gut feeling. One that comes from watching hours upon hours of footage just to sate my curiosity. Or perhaps it's hunger.

Either way, I'm here now. My methods for correctly assuming Zal would be outside will be my little secret.

"Can't sleep?" I ask.

It's a rhetorical question, of course. I know she can't. Her file might say as much, but the bags under her eyes are a dead giveaway.

Her eyes snap up to mine and her blanket falls as she jumps to her feet, arms raised like she's about to fight me.

PTSD is a real bitch.

She blinks a couple times before saying, "What are you doing here?"

I look around at the pool house, the pool, then the main house. "I believe I might own this place. One would say it affords me certain liberties with my property."

She gives me a blank look that gets me all excited. Her fire has returned. "Let me rephrase. Why have you left the warmth of your home when it's three in the morning?"

"A leisurely stroll?"

She purses her lips, silently saying, *try again*.

"It's a full moon. It's my duty as your employer to ensure that you are safe from all the night creatures."

We both glance up at the crescent moon. I guess that that's not very believable either.

I grin and help myself to the spot beside where she sat. Tapping the empty place next to me, I give her a bashful look. She narrows her eyes and considers for a moment before complying. The heat from her body seeps into the small space between us, and I want nothing more than to drag her closer to me.

I want her back.

It's a fact I've known since I was a teenager, and despite every change I've endured since she left, that is the only thing that has remained true.

I want Zalak back.

If she's picked up on my intentions, she hasn't let on. If there's a glimmer of reciprocation, she's hidden that just as well. I'll wait a lifetime if I have to.

The Zalak I knew from years ago and the one now wouldn't

take these kinds of advances for very long. I have to trust that her continued employment and residence on my property is an indication that maybe—just *maybe*—she wants me back too. I'll settle for knowing that she misses me.

And perhaps I'll take the old hoodie of mine that she's wearing as a sign as well.

"You know it's cold out here, right?" She catches my teasing smile, and I wrap her fallen blanket around her. To my surprise she doesn't throw it off.

That's a win in my books.

"I hadn't noticed," she deadpans.

"If you get a cold, I'd be a man—*woman*—down."

"As long as you follow protocol, I'm sure you'll survive."

Somehow, I don't think teasing her over how she cares about my safety will bode well. I'm going to tell myself that she cares about me because it's *me*, and not because she has to.

"Did you give all your supervisors this much attitude?"

"Fuck no."

I smirk. "Are you implying that I am not frightening?"

Zalak shrugs. "If you're willing to wake up at five in the morning to make me run drills, the fear factor might be taken up a notch."

I resist the urge to touch the cheek—the same soft skin I've kissed more times than I can count. "I'll have you know that everyone knows my name and the power I wield."

"*Mathijs Halenbeek*. Wow." She rolls her eyes. "It really strikes fear in my heart."

There she is.

I throw my head back and laugh. She chuckles alongside me—not the earth-shattering laugh I used to hear all the time. But it's closer than anything I've gotten in the past two months since she started accompanying me every time I leave the compound.

"It feels good," I say.

"What does?"

"To laugh again."

Neither of us adds to that. The slight curve of her lips makes me smile. I lean closer to her, relishing in the warmth of her proximity and the glimmer of light that's returned since she's come within my grasp.

After I lost my parents, I didn't think there was any semblance of good that would ever reappear in my life. My days continued. Men died. Green exchanged hands. Guns were fired. Day in and day out, all I could see was bleak misery.

The families living in the compound were the only sign of goodness. Even then, it was fleeting.

Year after year, I was kept up, wondering if Zalak felt the same way in the solitude of crowds. The lonesomeness of surface interactions. Did she ever see the insides of a person and think, *Is that it*? Did she stare at the ceiling and try to summon an image of a year from now and see nothing but the emptiness of existence?

I had hoped that wherever she was, she didn't feel those things. That she would look upon her sister and know the fire hasn't died out, and there's a reason to keep going.

When Zalak's team and Gaya died, the pain I felt wasn't from their deaths, it was from knowing that I might have lost her for good. I survived my parents' deaths because I wanted to make them proud, and I had Sergei by my side. What does Zalak have to keep her going?

When my personal guard died from a gunshot to the head—courtesy of Goldchild—I realized I had the perfect opportunity. She doesn't know it, but my men have orders to protect her with their lives, just as they would for me.

She needs the protection a lot less than I do. It turns me the hell on that she can beat someone up better than I can.

The Exodus might have reservations about accepting her into the fold, but I have no doubt she'll make a name for herself. One day, she'll have to prove to them that she's worthy of becoming a member. She's not ready for that kind of discussion yet, and there's still plenty of time before the Reckoning for me to tear down her walls just enough for her to let me in.

"Yes," Zalak says suddenly, catching me staring at her profile. "You asked me before if I can't sleep. The answer is yes."

I take her words to be the perfect opening, so I rise to my feet, then push the front door open, leaving her on the porch.

"What are you doing?"

I grin. "None of your business."

"I disagree since you're entering my place without permission."

"*Our* place, *Lieverd*," I correct.

Zalak shakes her head, leaving me to help myself to her things. Like all the other nights I've showed up at her door with dinner—which has been *many* times—the space is somewhat clean. It's nowhere near the standard of pristine cleanliness it was when she first moved in, and it's slowly getting messier as she gets more comfortable.

I grab the duvet and pillows off her bed and pile the spare blankets on top, then head back outside. The corners of her eyes crease as she watches me lay out the two blankets and arrange the pillows on the big lounger. I plop down in the chair, lie back, and toe my shoes off before kicking them up.

Grinning to myself, I take a second to admire her. Her oversized clothing is hiding all the muscle she's bulked up since moving here. I'll be honest, it makes my mouth water just thinking about it.

"Sit." I nod to the space beside me.

"I'm off the clock. You can't tell me what to do."

I grab my phone and fire off a text to her that I need her to work now. A text message sounds from inside, and the dirty side-eye she throws my way has me barking out a laugh.

Zalak pauses for a moment. Her eyes flash with an internal battle I can probably figure out. She's been closed off for so long, she needs to decide whether she's going to open herself back up. Even if she doesn't, I'll find a way to get in so her space is less lonely. I'll be the light in her dark corner whether she likes it or not.

Grumbling, she lowers herself beside me, all stiff and uncomfortable. This girl wouldn't do anything she doesn't want to do, and she's willingly entering into my space. I throw the many blankets on top of us and forgo the employer-employee decorum by wrapping my arm around her firm shoulders and pulling her to my side. If I thought she was tense before, this is a whole other category.

The frozen air turns our breaths into clouds, and yet I can't feel the chill. The tension that's knotted its way through my body slowly unwinds. Neither of us says a word, with her staring up at the sky, and me staring at her. When was the last time I held her in my arms? When was the last time it didn't feel so empty?

For the first time in years, it feels like everything is going to be okay. There are some things I'll never get back: habits, people, personality traits. But ten years later, and she still feels like a source of stability when everything is crumbling around me.

Before she came back, I stopped doing things because I wanted to, and only because I *had* to. Every transaction just felt like a job to put a tick in the book. Now there's a light I'm heading toward, not an endless loop.

The silence stretches between us, and with each passing minute, she slowly relaxes like she's letting herself accept this moment where she isn't out in the cold by herself.

"Remember when you'd sneak out while your parents were asleep?" I ask. We'd stay in one of the guesthouses located on the compound and do exactly what we're doing now; lounging beneath the stars.

Zalak huffs. "I can't believe I learned how to make a fake body in case Mom checked my room."

I'm just going to say it.

Her mom was a bitch.

Rest in peace.

"That skill comes in handy in my line of work. You should have added it to your resume."

She chuckles, leaning her head against my chest. In this moment, we're untouchable. There's no death, no war, no pit of despair waiting for us to drown in. But there are two things I know to be true.

She would kill for me, and I would do far worse for her.

CHAPTER 10

ZALAK

"How did I know I'd find you here?"

I glance away from the scope to Mathijs. I heard him coming through the forest a while back, but I let him pretend he was successfully sneaking up on me. "What gave me away? The cameras or the sound of gunshots?" It wouldn't be the former since I chose this spot blind spot.

"Neither. I just need to follow my heart to get to you."

Always such a flirt.

He drops on the blanket beside me, closer than would ever be acceptable in a professional setting. I try to ignore it, but there's no missing the way the distance between us—both physically and mentally—has been narrowing since I started working for him.

"That's so cringey," I say, attempting to disregard how his arm brushes against mine each time he breathes.

I have been in active war zones, for fuck's sake. Am I seriously losing focus because we're sort of touching?

Jesus Christ, Zalak. Get it together.

"Wait," Mathijs mumbles as he stares down the scope. His lips part, and the smooth skin of his forehead wrinkles. "You hit it?"

I scowl and grip the weapon tighter, then check the ballistics computer for its calculation. "I want a kill shot. That wouldn't have hit a vein."

I've been practicing every chance I get. It's a little hard to do when my only free time is at night, but I've been successfully fitting in at least four hours a week. To no one's surprise, Mathijs has refused to let me pay for the ammunition I'm using, claiming that it's for his benefit too.

Since our night on the front porch, he's been making time for me every single day. Sometimes it's for a quick break between work, or a full meal. Sometimes he joins me out here even though I'm certain there are a hundred more important things he could be doing.

Still, I can breathe a little easier when he's here. I just haven't figured out whether it's because it means he's alive and safe, or because I don't feel so alone. After two and a half years, I have someone to watch my six, and that is the most priceless thing Mathijs could give me.

Lining up the shot takes greater effort now that I have an

audience. Which is good. I need the added stress to keep me sharp. Inhaling deeply, I pull the trigger. My muscles solidify to withstand the recoil of the shot, and I keep my position to fire two more consecutive shots for good measure.

For fuck's sake. I missed. Again.

Great. Unless someone will die from a shot to the hip bone and another to the shoulder, my dreams are still just dreams.

"That's a good shot." His appraisal burns the side of my cheek.

"No. It isn't."

My breath hitches when he forgoes any claim that we're *accidentally* touching. His side presses up to mine, and he tucks a loose strand of hair behind my ear, lingering for a second too long, gliding his finger along the curve of my cheek like he's hypnotized by the contact. Heat explodes across my skin and I fight to keep my eyes open.

"You incapacitate them," he says, voice hoarse. "Then you kill them. That sounds like a good shot to me."

I blink, forcing myself out of my stupor and to the task at hand. Only, I can't concentrate. I can barely see the target at the other end of my scope. All because the hand that was just touching my cold skin is flat against the small of my back. A thick jacket separates us, but the heat of him seeps through the material like he's the purest form of fire.

For the sake of professionalism and everything we've been through these past ten years, I shouldn't let this keep going. I need to shuffle to the side, leave enough room for our sanity between us, and make it clear to him that there are boundaries in place that neither one of us should cross.

We've both had time to lick our wounds, but I'm still raw. I'll just bring him down with me. Plus, what if he decides he doesn't want me anymore? What if I wake up tomorrow without a job? I'm certain he won't do those two things, but still, there are so many compounding things that could make all of this blow up in our faces.

I need to put my foot down and tell him that we shouldn't be doing this.

But the best I can do is grunt in response. I'm a selfish, reckless woman. I don't want it to stop. I've missed feeling a body against mine. Missed feeling like there are two people on this earth and not just me.

I've missed *him*.

Mathijs leans in closer so his breath fans against my cheek, unfurling warmth throughout my body. My blood vibrates with anticipation, and for a second, I worry he can sense it radiating from me in waves. I don't need to look at him to see his mischievous smile. He's living for this.

"Try again," he whispers.

A shiver rolls down my spine. His voice is an octave deeper than usual, and every cell in my body sings from the sultry timbre. "Mathijs..."

"Yes, *Lieverd*?"

God. I don't know? Stop touching me? Keep touching me? I can't decide. This is wrong. Fucked up at a degree that I'm not sure I can accept. I'd be lying if I said I never saw this coming. He's been flirting with me since the very beginning, and not once has he acted anything but professional to every woman he's encountered.

Every single sign led here.

To him touching me.

To his lips inches away from mine.

We'll never be able to go back from whatever he's planning on doing. Nothing about this feels like an innocent tease, something to get a reaction out of me. It's not for thrills or out of boredom.

He wants whatever there is in the space between us. He's dying for what we were before I left. And if I'm being honest with myself, so am I. God, I want everything he's offering, and I'm selfish for it.

Rationally, I know I'll never be the person I was back then. I'll never wake up with a bounce in my step. I won't sit around and laugh with friends like I used to. There's no version of reality where either of us could ever be the teenagers who felt like we had our whole lives ahead of us.

But is it so wrong to want all of that? The taste of familiarity. To spend a couple minutes pretending like everything's okay. Like there is no war. There is no death. Just us, the open fields, and the taste of freedom. *Us.* I want us to happen again.

I want late nights under the stars, spontaneous adventures, and stupid jokes that have me snorting a laugh while Mathijs is rolling on the floor in tears. I want him.

Not as a means of distraction or a mindless pastime to make me feel something more than menial emotions. I want Mathijs now, the same way I wanted him before everyone around me died. I still think about him at night before I fall asleep. Still count down the moments until I can see him. Before working for him, I saw Mathijs in the faces of every man I went on hopeless dates with.

Every time I met someone who could have been my potential life partner, I asked myself one question: Would I risk it all for them?

The answer was always a resounding no.

But when I was fourteen, I was willing to risk my parents' wrath for Mathijs. I was eighteen and ready to face potential abandonment for him. Maybe I could have blamed those behaviors on my naivety, but I remember asking myself the same question a few years ago when I thought about him, and my answer was still yes. Just like I would have for Gaya and TJ. Now, I'm risking my life for him every day. I risk prison time. I risk death. I risk losing my sanity from a single trigger event.

Still, I'm here.

I take a deep breath and aim. It's harder to figure out the actual temperature when I feel like I've been set on fire. Mathijs's fingers dip beneath my clothes to span the width of my back. I close my eyes and relish in the feel of skin on skin. How long has it been since human touch hasn't hurt?

I pull the trigger. I don't think either of us knows whether I made it anywhere near the target, but I've stopped caring. All

I know is how his hands feel on me, and how the simple touch makes me close my eyes like I might be able to permanently etch this moment into my memories.

"Close," Mathijs mutters against my ear.

I bite the inside of my lip and attempt to line up the next shot—putting more effort in it this time. His ministrations make my concentration dwindle into dust. Once he dips the edges of his fingers into the waistband of my tights, I pull the trigger. I don't give a shit whether I've hit the human dummy or a real one.

Mathijs's chest vibrates against my shoulder as his hand curves around my waist, skating the line of my underwear as he goes. I squeeze my thighs to alleviate intensifying ache between my legs. I know I need to push him away, but I can't bring myself to because feeling wanted is the most addicting drug I've ever tasted.

I've learned how to hide in plain sight and not move a muscle while bullets fly my way. I've been trained not to speak if tortured. What I never thought I'd need to learn is how to stop myself from squirming.

"You just need to focus," he muses as his other hand snakes closer to my side until I can sense him a hair away from hitting the side of my breasts.

"You know what you're doing," I rasp, not letting myself look away from the scope.

"I'm helping," he says innocently. "Didn't they train you to stay perfectly still even when you're getting attacked? Show me how good you are at it." Soft, pillowy lips brush against my cheek, and I fight the urge to turn to kiss him. I wonder if he's still a gentle kisser, or if life has hardened him into steel. Has he grown possessive over the years? Turned down the path of needing to claim?

I can't ever know. Kissing him seems like acceptance, and I don't know if I'm ready for that just yet.

"Show me why you're one of the greatest snipers alive."

His fingers breach my waist band until his entire hand is pressed against my lower stomach. My legs part involuntarily, and I internally chastise myself for being so needy. But God, I can't help it. I didn't realize how much I've been craving this type of intimacy.

"Watch your form, Zalak."

Fuck.

I suck in a sharp breath to block out the spell he's casting on me, but there's no fighting the fact that his fingers are inching lower with every heartbeat. The ringing in my ears grows louder, and I'm shivering from the feel of finally having his hands back on me.

My hips buckle when he strums my clit, and desire pools between my legs, saturating the thin material of my panties.

"You flinched." He *tsks*. "You can do better than that."

Fruitlessly, I try to remember the calculation for the shot. Has the direction of the wind changed? Gone down?

The next strum of his fingers makes me lean my head against the rifle. Nothing could have prepared me for this. Pleasure bursts in each corner of my body and a low keening sound starts at the base of my throat.

"Shh," Mathijs whispers, torturing me with the way he rubs in slow, purposeful circles, as if he remembers just how I like it. "You don't want to give away our location now, do you?"

I think I might kill him.

"Is there something wrong?" he taunts while I struggle to keep myself still.

A *bang* goes off with the pull of the trigger. When I flinch, it has nothing to do with the recoil, and everything to do with the finger he slips inside me.

Jesus *fuck* it's been a long time since anyone has touched me there. If I had any hope of shutting this down before, it's all gone now.

He hums, pumping into me in agonizingly slow movements. I squeeze my eyes shut and groan, arching to take him in deeper. "You really shouldn't be so distracted when operating a firearm, darling. Do you know how dangerous that is?"

My pussy clamps around his finger and my eyes flutter open, and I grip the gun to stop myself from grinding into his hand. I shouldn't be anywhere near a rifle with how disconnected my brain has become to reality. Someone could walk by, and I don't think I'd care right now. Hell, I don't think I'd even care if I accidentally shot someone. But something else makes me pause, and once the idea takes hold, there's nothing I can do to dispel it.

There's this one other disturbing thought circling my head:

I want him to fuck me.

I need to forget how to spell my own name. I need him to make me go nonverbal with how thoroughly he's fucking me. His fingers aren't enough. There are too many layers between us and it's becoming harder to stay put than it is to start moaning out his name.

But my self-control is fried anyway.

I'll deal with the aftermath of this later. For now, we're just two people.

I push my hips against his, needing to feel that I'm affecting him just as much as he's affecting me. The truth of it is evident in the hard bulge that meets me. I bite down on a scream when his fingers plunge inside of me, pummeling like he's wanting to send me into an early grave.

My eyes roll to the back of my head. Every atom in my body is vibrating with pleasure.

I barely notice my surroundings. Hell, everything on the other side of the scope is a blur. The lusty haze over my vision has impaired every one of my senses, and it only gets worse with my nearing climax. Still, I want *more*.

Would it be so bad if we went there? I'm a grown woman. Sex doesn't have to mean more than just sex.

The pressure in my core builds with every drive of his fingers. I'm nothing more than a wet, panting mess, silently begging to be stretched out on his cock. I need to feel him more than I need air. I can't remember what it's like to have Mathijs take me like there's no other person on this Earth for him, and I think I'll die if I don't get the reminder. Soon.

I gasp when he suddenly pulls out his fingers and shoves my pants down my hips. Automatically, I arch my back to grant him easier access. I'm so desperate for him and everything he has to offer—sexual and otherwise—but I'm so fucking scared of what might come next.

For one heavy moment, I think he'll realize what a bad idea this is and walk away. We'll go on pretending like nothing ever happened, and I'll live the rest of my life regretting that I didn't say something or *do* something—*anything*—to show him how much I care about him. That I appreciate him. That I never stopped loving him.

With one kiss against my shoulders, all my worries vanish. I shiver from the warmth of his hands groping my ass. Slowly, he pushes my panties to the side, like he's waiting for me to put a stop to this. I answer with the raise of my hips, and something tangible passes over us.

Mathijs straddles my thighs with his, blocking out the cold, and yanks a cry out of me when he fills me in one fell swoop. Whatever stretch I felt around his fingers is nothing compared to the ecstasy of this. It's everything I could hope for and more.

"*Fuck*," he groans at the same time I buckle forward. It's a miracle the sniper hasn't fallen out of my hold. "Why'd you stop? Take the shot."

My fingers shake as I grip the rifle and bring it back into position. It's impossible to line it up when my vision is so hazy. Now, I don't think I'll even make it in the general direction of the target. Each roll of his hips rocks me forward. If it weren't for all the time I spent sitting in the back of a truck, gun aimed, the sniper would have flown from my fingers a long time ago.

The shot rings through the clearing. Little gasps force out of me with each one of his thrusts. All I can hear are the lewd, wet sounds as he slams into me.

"You're doing so well, *Lieverd*." His voice is husky as his hand moves beneath my shirt to cup my breast. "Just pretend I'm not even here."

My nails dig into the metal of the weapon at the way he twists my nipple. I'm breaking every single cardinal rule of using firearms, because I point at a tree less than half a mile away and shoot. The bullet hits the very center of it. Bark explodes everywhere from the use of long-distance ammo on a close shot.

Mathijs's pace becomes more relentless, more desperate. As if seeing me handle a gun is making him lose his mind. The realization of it hits me like a ton of bricks, and my lungs seize. Every part of me does. The orgasm rips through me without warning. The cry that tears past my lips echoes between the trees.

I don't bother trying to stop my moans. I even give up holding the weapon while my eyes roll to the back of my head and I fall to the ground to lift my hips to meet him thrust for thrust.

All it takes is the pinch of my nipples and the push of my lower back against the blanket, and blinding light impairs my vision. Liquid white heat burns through my veins. My core spasms and tightens around him, prolonging my orgasm to a point where I can't figure out which way is up and which is down.

Dots dance behind my eyes as his thrusts become animalistic. I swear I can taste him at the back of my throat. He finishes with a groan, spilling his come into me. Mathijs's hands land on either side of my head, and a laugh bubbles out of him as he presses a kiss against my temple. "*Ik ben duizend keer voor je gevallen, Lieverd.*"

I frown, unsure what he's saying. He was never the best at speaking Dutch, but it never stopped him from trying. Either way, I try to get ahold of my trembling body, but my clit is so sensitive, even the breeze feels too damn much. At the same time, the only thing that would make this perfect is if I could close my eyes and fall asleep with him still inside me. The exhaustion of life and sex has rendered my bones numb, but right now, I could almost fool myself into believing that whatever comes next will be easy.

"Did you get the shot?" he asks, still on top of me.

We both grab a scope and look through it. I still at the same time he barks out a laugh.

I hit the target in the balls.

CHAPTER 11

ZALAK

It's pretty.

Too pretty.

That word and I are no longer acquainted. It feels wrong to use it, let alone wear the lie.

Cold sweat snakes down my spine at the thought of seeing Mathijs. I don't regret what we did in the woods two days ago. But it was inevitable that something would shift between us after taking the plunge. I don't know where to go from here, and... I don't think I can stay here anymore.

When I saw him yesterday, he practically had a skip in his step. This afternoon he was basically wearing heart-eyed sunglasses. It made my heart double in size and brought back feelings of hope and contentment. Maybe there is something good in store for me. Maybe I've gotten over my fears. Maybe I'm the same person I was before everything blew up.

Maybe. Maybe. Maybe.

But everything good comes crashing down.

I stare at the text from Mathijs again.

> Mathijs: There's a dress for you in front of your door. Wear it. I need you to accompany me to a dinner date tonight.

Not *accompany him as his date*.

Not just *accompany* him to a meeting.

He's getting me dressed up so I can sit there and watch him have his date. The pit in my stomach makes me nauseous. This is the very last thing I expected from him, and I feel so fucking stupid for letting him in when he never intended on staying. Never in a million years did I think he would be capable of such a cruel thing. He's changed in a way that I don't like.

Jesus Christ, he fucked me in the middle of the woods just two damn days ago. Now he's gallivanting around, parading another woman in front of me?

We may not be exclusive anymore but I sure as shit don't deserve this. The text and this dress are reminders that I'm the damaged help. I'm a hired gun. An easy lay. Nothing more.

I have never felt so dehumanized before. Part of me wants to hurt him for hurting me. The other part is saying that this was always how it was meant to be, and that I deserve this pain. The last part—the practical part—is saying that this is it. I need to stay professional and it's my fault for getting my emotions involved.

Really, I should never have let it get this far. The second he put his hand on me, I should have drawn the line. Now look where it's gotten me. Accompanying my ex to his motherfucking date when I had his come dripping out of me less than forty-eight hours ago.

I just need to be here for another month, then I'll be able to leave and get a job in another city. Forget all about the past few months working for him, and how it's made me feel more like a living, breathing human.

So I don't hate him for the reminder when his charity is the main reason I've been getting out of bed in the morning lately.

One night of watching him wine and dine another woman won't kill me. And if he sends me a midnight message asking if I feel like hanging out? I'll deal with it. Professionalism will be my middle name. I've been through a hell of a lot worse.

Swallowing my pride, I put on the ridiculously pretty forest-green outfit Mathijs left for me. It's the most impractical getup he could ever get his bodyguard to wear. There's zero way I could put up a good fight in it.

It's a struggle to zip up the satin bandeau by myself, but the chiffon wrap skirt is easy enough to work out. The final article of clothing is another piece of chiffon fabric that I can't work out. This entire outfit has to cost at least a weeks' salary. There's intricate beading all over it and heavy gold bangles, earrings, and arm cuffs that suffocate my biceps and make me look somewhere north of a million bucks.

I slip my arm through the cutout and pull the other side over my head so the fabric drapes across my body from one shoulder, displaying the sun tattooed on my shoulder and the tiger crawling down my forearm.

What kind of establishment are we going to that requires this level of grandeur? I look more like I'm going to a ball than a dinner I'm playing security at. This dress is hardly practical if I have to chase someone down. Honestly, how in the fuck does he expect me to ride a bike in this dress?

I throw on some makeup, strap a gun and a knife to my thigh, then hide another in the matching gold purse. Here's to hoping that there won't be any pat downs where we're going. I'm not on board with guarding from a distance while weaponless, and I might throw up if I have to be close by while he schmoozes another woman. Here's to also hoping that I can get a sweet middle.

Why was there no warning for our team to scope out the place first?

Why the *hell* does he need me to be there while he flirts up some woman who, by all accounts, was made for this type of world? Maybe she's going to be my future employer.

Grinding my teeth, I throw on my coat and try not to stomp up to the main house in my heels. *Heels.* Is he kidding me?

Fuck this.

I should suggest that this is a task Sergei would be more suitable to because I can't stand there and watch—*no*. I can do this. I'm a *professional*. I survived a goddamn bomb that killed my best friend, then lost my sister a couple of days later. I lost my sister and best friend in the same week.

This? It's nothing. *Nothing*.

I school my expression and will my body to relax, even though the only mode of transport will be the SUV, just to make matters abundantly worse than they already are. There's no use wasting energy convincing myself that maybe we'd take a helicopter to the destination, or something equally as absurd. My only hope is to convince myself that *I'm not back there*.

The car isn't going to explode.

No one is going to die.

TJ can't die again.

Gaya is already gone.

I'll be fine.

I make eye contact with Sergei as soon as I enter the foyer to ascend the stairs to Mathijs's office.

"Outside," is all the head of security says.

Swallowing the building panic, I nod at the door. I would take the juvenile jealousy and disappointment over this bone-deep fear clawing through my soul. I keep repeating the useless assurances to myself as I climb down the front steps toward the convoy. My knees wobble with the closing distance, but the call of my name makes me stop and change course toward Mathijs.

My mind flashes with memories of our time in the forest, and an ache starts in my core.

He's glowing. He has been since we... *rekindled*. His smile

142

is so bright, I almost stumble back from the shock. Dressed in a suit that makes him look straight out of a magazine, every inch of him is styled to utter perfection. Every strand of hair is exactly where it's meant to be. I always thought that he's the most attractive man that I've ever laid my eyes on. Seeing him beam the way he is now... no one will ever compare. Whatever beauty he has is rooted inside him as well.

But he isn't mine.

Mathijs smirks knowingly as he stands next to the neon green Bugatti.

I stare at it for a moment in an attempt to work out why it's out of the garage. The realization makes me glare at him.

He's so damn hard to keep alive.

"As your security, I would advise against driving in this vehicle. *Separately*. Anyone could corner you," I say.

"Surely they have to catch me first."

"The windows—"

"Are bulletproof."

"You could be followed."

"I will be followed." He points to the four SUVs behind us.

There's no winning this argument. He's still the boss and he makes the final decision. Even if it means it might end up with him killed. Maybe I'll drag Sergei into this discussion so he can be the voice of reason. I nod and move to turn around, but pause.

"Zalak."

I look over my shoulder and raise a brow at him just as he

holds the passenger door open. "How are you meant to protect me if you're in another car?"

My stomach convulses at the prospect of getting into a car, but the fear dissipates when I eye the Bugatti.

It's... it isn't raising my hackles. The car is so small and low to the ground that my brain isn't reconciling the vehicle in front of me to the one I almost died in. The neon color removes the connection to the event, and any possibility that it might be one in the same as an armored car. This seems more like a scene from a movie than a memory.

I clear my throat and thank him as I take my seat in the car.

Nothing. No cold sweats. No shaking.

He closes the door behind me. My heart hammers as I take in the interior. Still nothing. It's like I'm willing the panic to take hold, but it never does. The air doesn't grow thinner. My skin doesn't burn. There's no ringing in my ears.

I'm... I'm okay.

Jesus fucking Christ, I'm actually alright.

I could almost laugh at the thought. I'm inside a car, and I'm *fine*. Nothing is happening to me. There's no bomb about to hit this tin can. I could almost kiss Mathijs for this.

The beast purrs awake and my lips stretch into the slightest smile. I'm doing it. I'm actually fucking doing it. Mathijs takes his seat, and I repress the urge to tell him I haven't stepped foot into something other than a bus, jet, or a limo since I touched down back in the US. Now here I am, sitting in the front seat of a car, dressed up, sober, and *with an actual job*.

Wherever Gaya and TJ are, they better be having a cold one for me.

Mathijs winks at me like he's silently celebrating with me. There's barely a moment of hesitation before he speeds down to the end of the drive, forgetting all about his security detail. My hand automatically drops to the door handle—not for show. He drives like a lunatic. It's a stretch to say he "looked" both ways before tearing onto the road.

"You're a liability," I mutter.

He turns toward me, lips splitting into a boyish grin as he drives us single-handedly. "I have to keep my men on their toes."

"Eyes on the road," I snap. "I'm having a hard time protecting you from yourself." He chuckles and does as he's told, but before he can respond, I ask the burning questions. "Where are we going?"

"To a dinner."

"Where?"

"A restaurant."

I glare at his profile. "*Where*, Mathijs?"

He sighs and smiles wider as if the thought of our destination makes him excited. My gut sours, putting a lid on whatever joy I felt moments before.

"A Michelin-star restaurant with a six-month waitlist. I have a private room booked."

So he can have privacy with his date.

I roll down the windows to let the cool air circulate through the two-seater car. His date might be sitting in this very spot a couple hours from now, and I'll be forced to find my way back.

"Who are you meeting?"

"You'll see."

My stomach lurches when we go around a bend. Or maybe it's because I haven't seen him so at ease since I started working for him. There's no tension lining his shoulders. The creases around his eyes are from age rather than concern. He's in his element, and I wish I could just blame it on the exhilaration from racing through the city.

He's meeting another woman and he's going to make me watch.

Maybe I'd handle this a whole lot better if he told me the whole purpose of this meeting is to get information regarding Goldchild. That this is all a ruse. But neither of those things are true and it kills me.

The bright lights of the restaurant loom ahead, and I scan the area, noting the other establishments dotted along the street, and the many patrons who've decided to eat out on a Thursday night. It's an upscale area of town, and though I spot some security around, I'd wager that none of them will be of any use if things go south—which is entirely possible, since this area is known for its criminal underbelly: illegal gambling rings, Mafia-owned restaurants, and a club rumored to be owned by the Bratva. It's a shitshow waiting to happen.

I glance behind us, knowing without looking that none of Mathijs's men will be near because we drove two times the speed limit to get here.

Great. I'm on my own. The only leg up I have is the fact that I look more like his date than someone who's here to keep watch over someone. A-plus for blending in, I guess.

Mathijs pulls up in front of the valet, and he runs around to open my door before the attendant can do it. He offers me his hand, and I hesitate before accepting it. He passes the key along, then places his hand on my lower back to steer me toward the host.

"This isn't a good look if you're on a date," I whisper just as we're about to reach the front desk.

"Oh no," he says with faux sadness. "My date can't come. I guess you'll have to keep me company instead."

My lips part and heat colors my skin. He… That little shit.

"There was never any date, was there?"

He moves behind me to remove my coat once we reach the front desk, then hands the jacket to the host to put away. Mathijs circles me, giving me his full attention, and my cheeks heat under his hungry stare and from all the spiraling I've done this afternoon. Of course he would never have done something like that to me. I should have had faith in him.

But in my defense, he acted like a cryptic asshole.

His eyes darken when they land on mine, then he roves over the rest of me. The look of pure adoration and need that paints his features has my hairs standing on end. It's the type of stare that tells me tonight is full of promises.

"I don't know what you're talking about. Are you not my date? You came here with me. And you made yourself absolutely…" My heart stutters as he trails a single finger along my jaw and leans closer to my ear. "*Delectable.* Just for me."

The air sucks out of me as he pulls away and takes my hand in his to lead us in the direction of the private room. I'm too gobsmacked by the situation to remember that I'm still on the clock. Technically. I don't notice any of the people around us or the number of exits in the room or any blind spots. My focus is solely on him and the easy smile he wears.

First, I rode in a car without issue. Now, I'm having a date. With Mathijs. While carrying several weapons. Ten years after I said goodbye to him. Those aren't sentences I thought I'd ever string together.

Ever the gentleman, he pulls out a chair for me and I finally take in the room we have all to ourselves. The lack of cameras is the first thing I notice. Renaissance paintings hang on the mahogany walls, and there are flower arrangements and statues sitting atop marble pedestals. In the middle of it all is our rectangular table, the white tablecloth, and the fine china.

The murmurings of patrons can only *just* be heard above the strings playing through the room. Based on the volume difference between the main dining area and ours, I'd say some soundproofing is at play.

Mathijs orders us a bottle of wine while I scrutinize the single exit in and out of the room. I won't pretend to know whether what he ordered is white or red, and where on the pH scale it might sit. His mom used to tell me all about the various undertones, acidity, and how to make it. Not that I remember any of it. At the ripe age of sixteen, she'd sit me down to do tastings and she'd let me have just enough to get tipsy. No one was any wiser when I got home.

The waiter leaves after taking our meal orders and serving our drinks, so the only two souls in this room are him and I. The quiet amplifies until it's hard to breathe. It's hard to look at him and see how at ease he is on his chair, lounging back like nothing could faze him. His clothes hug his lean frame, and pull taut when he reaches for the glass.

Mathijs's stare is on me, so heated I'm pretty sure he's undressed me without laying a hand on me.

I chew on my bottom lip. This is too soon, right? Too much? He knows what's wrong with me, and he hasn't run for the hills. That's a sign that I can just go along with this and see where this leads, right?

We crossed a line that can't be uncrossed, and he's taking us for a plunge. I've come a long way, but I don't know how ready I am to commit when I've only just found my footing again—literally and figuratively.

"Is something wrong?" he asks, brows furrowing.

Taking a less than healthy gulp of wine to clear my throat, I steel my spine to face him. "We're moving quickly."

"My come was dripping out of your pussy two days ago. I'd call this catching up."

Lord, give me strength. Red flushes my skin, but I keep my composure, clutching the stem of the wineglass. "You never asked me if I wanted to go to dinner with you. What makes a date a date is both people agree and are aware it's happening."

Would I have agreed if he asked? Probably not. I'm sure I would have made some excuse about security risks with Goldchild, and beat around the bush about the real reason I'm resisting. I'm not ready—which, if I'm being truthful, I have no idea what that looks like.

"I wholeheartedly agree." His lips tip to one side in a cocky smirk. "That's why I haven't labeled all the other times we've had dinner together as a 'date,' and why you were given prior warning this time. See, you're even all dressed up for it."

I blink. "You told me I was accompanying you to a date."

"Point and case; I told you." He smirks.

"You gave me this dress and told me to wear it."

"Ah yes. You have never denied an order."

"Within reason, I will. I was assuming I was getting appropriately dressed for an occasion within my job description."

Mathijs arches a brow. "Are you implying that I could get a bag packed and you'd hop on a plane and accompany me to Costa Rica? Bikinis, short skirts, and summer dresses."

No. That's definitely not what I'm implying. Outside of a professional setting at least. "So long as the correct security measures are in place and every detail is planned appropriately."

He sighs. "You're no fun. Where's your spontaneity?"

"Your impulsiveness *and* recklessness have left you without a full security detail."

"Untrue." He sips his wine and nods toward my purse. "You're armed."

"Am I your guard or your date?"

"You're murderous, and stunning. You could be neither of those things and still kill a man with your bare hands. So take your pick. Either way, you're coming home with me tonight."

I huff. "We live on the same property, Mathijs. It doesn't count."

The waiter returns with our food and we thank him. I quietly dig into the meal I would have preferred takeout over. I subtly watch him chewing away like he's deep in thought—which is never a good thing.

Back when we were younger, that look meant that he was about to stir trouble or say something he shouldn't. Usually both.

I throw back more expensive wine that's completely wasted on me, only to freeze when he pushes his cutlery to the side so the space in front of him is bare.

Definitely not good.

"Perhaps I'll explain this a different way—and you'll have to excuse my language," he says with an air of professionalism I'm unused to. "I am about to eat a four-hundred-dollar, world-renowned meal, when I'd rather have you splayed out on the table with my head between your thighs because I am utterly *ravished*. We were never *done*. We were always meant to come back to each other. So you can decide whether you're here for work or pleasure; just know that the latter will be on the table tonight." He nods to my plate. "So, *Lieverd*, eat. I have no intention of ordering dessert."

I'm at a loss for words. A blaze of fire scorches a path across my skin. An ache forms between my legs at the memory of having him inside of me. Knowing that a repeat of those events is on the menu only drenches me to the point I have to shift in my seat to get some much needed friction.

"Is that confidence, self-assurance, or blatant entitlement?" I manage to pull myself together to reply.

"I assure you, I understand the word *no* in twenty-three different languages. You want honesty, I'll give you honesty. We have both come too far to speak in riddles. You're mine. I'm yours. That's how it was before, and how it is tonight, tomorrow, and every day after that. Now"—he pushes a small platter toward me—"are these oysters going to waste tonight?"

I don't answer. My breath comes out harsh and uneven as I eye the food between us. Every rule of etiquette is telling me to say thank you, but for both of our sakes, we should stop it now. The last thing he needs is more baggage, and the last thing I need is to risk falling again when I don't feel solid yet.

But I'm a selfish woman. Lying in that clearing with him inside me was the first time I felt *truly* alive. It was like I finally became one with my senses. I could smell the crisp air, hear the chipper of birds, and feel the damp earth beneath me. I wasn't just aware of all of it—I *appreciated* life. I want that again. I'll deal with the fallout that comes later. Tonight, I want a chance to feel human again.

I keep darting my eyes between the porcelain and Mathijs's hypnotic green eyes. Before I can make a decision, Mathijs's voice comes out, deep and filled with the type of dark desire that makes a woman fall onto her knees.

"Take out your gun, Zalak."

My gaze snaps up to his. "What?"

He motions to my purse. "Your gun. Put it on the table."

I hesitate for a moment before doing as he says. There's a barely audible *thud* when the handgun hits the wooden table. Something about the command weaves threads of desire with my blood.

He shrugs off his jacket, loosens his tie, then rolls the sleeves of his white top up to his elbows.

"Dismantle it."

Rationally, I know I should ask questions. Maybe even refuse to do it because of the risks we face. But my racing pulse dares to do nothing of the sort. I do exactly as he says. I lay out each piece on the table and wait for the next command.

"Put it back together without the magazine."

This time, I frown but comply, shifting in my seat to generate any kind of pressure. Lust is a living, breathing entity inside of my veins. It turns everything into various shades of red.

"Make sure there are no bullets in there, darling. I'm going to fuck you with it."

My lips part. That's... No, he didn't mean that, right?

Mathijs leans back in the chair and places his hands on either side of the armrest as if he were a king, and I was one of his loyal subjects ready to serve his every whim. There's only just enough room between him and the table.

Shuddering, I double check there's nothing inside the chamber so there's no chance of any kind of misfire.

His gaze drops to the empty space on the table in front of him. "Sit and spread your legs for me."

A tremor works its way through my limbs as I cautiously rise to my feet and stalk toward him. He watches me like I'm the prey and he's the real predator among us. Green eyes drop to my lips when I lick them. They blow out into an endless void of black as my fingers travel down to my thighs to inch the skirt up to allow me enough movement to part my legs.

The cutlery clatters when I make it to the edge of the table and place my feet on his armrest, just beneath his hands. Slowly, I find the courage to part my knees and let the gauzy fabric fall back to give him a clear view. My breathing stutters from the heat of his gaze, while his stops altogether.

His hands follow the undersides of my legs, up to my hips, before grabbing the tactical knife strapped to my thigh. I gasp when the cold metal caresses my hot skin right before the thin material of my panties rip apart with the slightest tug of the blade.

From this angle, I can see the evidence of my arousal dripping from me and onto the table. The sound of approval that comes from him sends a bolt of warmth unfurling around my heart. "You look good enough to eat, *Lieverd*."

I bite down on the inside of my cheek when he trails his fingers along the seams of my inner thighs, making my legs quiver and fight to snap close. My eyelids grow heavy, and I grip the tablecloth to stop myself from pushing my hips closer to

SCORPION

him when he leans down and places a kiss to the inside of my knee. He doesn't need to know how desperate I am for him.

"Do you know how long I've been starving?"

Mathijs drags his lips halfway up my thigh, then kisses a path to my core, only to pause an inch away from where I need him most. A needy whimper pulls out of me because his promise feels too good, and I'm losing control over my frayed edges.

"A man should never be left unfed for so long," he rasps.

His hot breath fans over my center, and I give up trying to stop myself from angling my body to where I want him to go. I throw my head back with a moan when he licks the full length of my pussy. Once. Like he's playing with his food.

"We can get... *creative*. You don't want to know all the ways I've been imagining you."

A string of curses flies past my lips when his mouth returns to where I'm aching the most. His tongue flicks out, lapping at me. From the way his fingers dig into the meat that hugs my curves to the way his eyes bore up at me like I had it all wrong earlier.

I am not his loyal subject: he's mine.

Soft moans mix with the string music, and my desire warms the air around while he consumes me so completely, it's hard to believe I haven't become a corpse.

Mathijs's tongue moves side to side over my clit, winding the muscles in my core tighter like I could combust at any second. He pulls away too soon, wearing the evidence of my arousal on his face.

"I'm a respectable man, darling," he says, voice hoarse like he's barely holding on. "And you make me want to do things to you that will make me lose that title."

A groan builds in the back of my throat when he slips two fingers inside of me and curls them. Stars burst behind my vision and the world tips on its axis.

"Your gun," he rasps.

I fumble behind me until my hand lands on the weapon. I pass it to him faster than necessary, then lean back in an open invitation for him to do whatever the hell he wants as long as he can get rid of the soul-consuming ache building within me.

Mathijs removes his fingers to replace them with the cool tip of the gun. If I hadn't already been discharged from the military, they sure as shit would discharge me now. My eyes gloss over at the hard intrusion, but I spread my legs wider to welcome it deeper, and he watches every one of my reactions with the intensity of someone whose life depends on the very act.

Inch by inch, he slides it further inside me, slowly spinning it so the trigger guard pushes against my clit for added stimulation. Moisture glistens on the weapon as he draws it out of me, then pushes it back in with agonizingly slow speed. The stretch adds to the pure bliss coursing through my veins. I'm going to come if he keeps this up.

"Look at me or I'll stop."

I avert my bleary gaze up to his ungodly expression, which is an unholy mixture of languish, desperation, frustration, and lust. Seeing him out of sorts because of me has my toes curling with self-satisfaction. He's just as helpless to this pull as I am.

Before I can make another sound, his lips descend on mine, capturing me in the type of kiss I thought was only possible in dreams. I meet him with the same fervor and reverent worship. Like he said, I *am* his. I just don't know how to be.

If we were crossing a line two days ago, we're jumping straight off a cliff tonight. This is a point of no return. *Acceptance*. Whatever hell we're in, we're agreeing to be in it together. Every dark, depraved skeleton buried in the recesses of our minds are to be held by each other. Somehow, someway. It's just us.

The logical part of me is jumping up and down about my job. I refuse to be put to the side just because he doesn't want to risk my safety for the sake of his. I'm good at what I do and there's no relationship that will get in the way of that. I won't let it. I built this life. I honed my skills. When I get lowered into a grave, it's the only thing that I can say was truly my own.

With the next drive of the gun, I'm gasping for breath and clawing at his back. "Right there."

He does it again.

Over and over until I can barely hold my weight anymore. Each time the trigger guard hits my clit, another curse falls past my lips. The orgasm knocks the wind out of my lungs and renders me limp and shaking on the table as he continues to drive the gun into me.

Mathijs captures my lips like he wants to steal the sound from me. He doesn't give me any reprieve before unzipping his pants and thrusting into me. My body sings from the change in sensation. It hits me far deeper than the gun, and has the perfect curve that reaches the spot that makes the lights in my head go out.

"Ik kan niet zonder jou."

I nod even though I don't understand a word of what he's saying. I'm so sensitive, it almost hurts to keep going. But I would rather die than stop this. My second orgasm looms closer with each of his thrusts, and I claw at his back, begging for more.

His lips are on me. His hands. His eyes. Every single part of him moves like it belongs to me. Like it always has, and he's begging me to see it.

A trickle of fear crawls through the lusty haze. I don't know if I'm ready to go around declaring to the world that we're in a relationship. But he's given me the push I needed to stop looking at my own reflection. Mathijs forced me out of my shell and gave me a roof, food, and companionship.

I know if I told him to stop, he would. If I said I needed time before any kind of relationship, he'd give it to me. If I wanted space... I don't know how willing he'd be for that. But I'm sure he'd keep me at a distance.

So this time, when I kiss him, I hope he knows how grateful I am for helping me back onto my feet. I hope he's aware that with each move of my lips, I'm thanking him for all his insistence. I tell him with my lips that he will always have my endless gratitude for reminding me what it means to be alive. *Living*. Not just a shadow of my former self.

I don't want to say that I owe him for taking me in when he

didn't have to, but there's no doubt in my mind that I would put myself in the line of fire for him. I'll do it every day until I can't stand anymore.

His groan ripples between us, breaths growing more labored like he's on the pinnacle of his own release. The pressure of his thumb against my clit pulls me closer to the edge of another release that I don't know how I'll survive.

He murmurs words in Dutch that I don't understand, and I capture his bottom lip between my teeth. A noise that doesn't sound human rumbles at the back of his throat and his thrusts turn punishing. Blinding. Completely soul-destroying. The grip he has around the back of my neck is hard enough to leave behind a splotch of blue and black on my skin.

"Please don't stop," I whisper, clawing at any part of him I can reach while his thumb circles my clit.

"*Louder*," he growls.

I whimper when he slams into me. My hand flies behind me to keep me steady. My moans come out unbidden and uncaring for the audience outside. By some miracle, I manage to form the words he wants, and they come out closer to a chant that builds the pressure in my core until I hit a breaking point. Every inch of me shatters and reforms, crying out his name like it's my only link to life.

His own climax hits right after mine, and he seals it with a kiss that could stop time itself. Everything about it feels like utter perfection; the way his come drips into me, our thundering heartbeats, the desperate touches.

But the words that follow feel like a pin drop in a quiet room. Something about it is so vulnerable, yet feels like I'm being gutted alive.

"Let me make you another promise. One day, you will finally be my wife."

CHAPTER 12

ZALAK

I sway, unsure whether to feel giddy from bliss, exhausted from having my insides wrung dry, or hollow now that I've become aware of reality.

I don't have the energy to feel embarrassed as we navigate between the tables. Anyone could have heard us. I'm sure I look like I've just been fucked within an inch of my life, but the opinions of strangers are far too insignificant and inconsequential in the grand scheme of things.

At least my instincts were functioning enough to fully assemble the gun and have it safely tucked away in my handbag before we exited the room. Sergei and the rest of the team are out front waiting for us to come out.

Mathijs's hand rests at the base of my spine, while my own

clutches my purse. The weight of the gun keeps me somewhere between feeling invincible and like death is around the corner. It's a toxic combination that keeps me grounded enough to not gawk at Mathijs over his promise.

His wife.

I thought about it all the time when we were younger—including the two kids we'd have, the low-key wedding, and the summer home in a cottage on the mountains that we'd escape to when the city got too loud. I once told him my life plans: the age I expected us to marry, and that we'd only consider children when we neared our thirties so we'd both have established careers first.

Thinking about putting a ring on my finger seems like such a foreign concept that could never happen to someone like me. When I left home, I debated whether I wanted to swear off marriage, but decided against it because I didn't want my mother to control my life. Although, being on board about it feels like I'm letting her shove her values in my face while saying *I told you so*.

But the woman is dead.

They all are.

Everything from here on out is up to me. People come and go, either alive or dead.

I just need to get my shit together.

Taking in a deep breath, I draw my shoulders back. If I need time, Mathijs will give it. If I ask for space, he'll put me at arm's length. Nothing is going to go wrong.

"How was your meal?" the hostess asks as she hands us our

coats.

Mathijs grins and casts me a sideways glance. "Delicious."

I scoff quietly and approach the valet to wait for his Bugatti. The cold air shocks me out of the postcoital bliss and near existential crisis, enough for me to scan our surroundings for threats. Sergei and the rest of the men are across the street—except for the one guy who has stationed himself a couple meters away in case I need assistance.

The neon green car pulls up in front of me just as Mathijs reaches my side.

"Shall we?" His lips are split into a dazzling smile that shifts my equilibrium. Transporting me back to the private dining room when we were both finding God.

He winks like he knows exactly what I'm thinking about. I shake my head to knock some composure into me. But I don't react soon enough.

A shot rings out. Glass shatters behind me. Screams ensue above the roar of an engine. Metal groans. And for the briefest moment, I freeze.

I'm back there. Watching TJ die. Watching them all die.

A second fire hits the wall near me, and I spring into action. I grab Mathijs by the scruff of his neck and shove him to the ground behind the car. My muscles seize and my lungs contract, blurring the environment around me so I'm caught between a scorching desert and reality.

I can't hear anything beyond the ringing in my ears. I'm only slightly aware of the carnage from the debris flying through the air.

I grab my gun and fire back at the three cars and motorbikes driving by. I can't count how many guns are pointed our way because of the film over my vision. I can't even make out faces. They could be masked for all I know.

My mind flips from the Middle East to the humid wetlands in Asia and South America. To the burning armored car in Senegal.

Over and over.

Jungle. Forest. Sand.

Movement beside me pulls me from the mirage, but it isn't enough for me to recognize who it is or what they're doing. I keep pulling the trigger. Again. And again. And again. Jungle. Forest. Sand.

I run onto the street to chase them down. When I'm out of ammo, I reach beneath my skirt to draw the spare gun, but someone stops me. I throw my arm out and manage to stop just before landing a blow.

He's familiar. I *know* him. Where do I know him from? His lips move, but I can't hear what he's saying. I'm sure I've seen his face a thousand times before. But I don't recognize him. I don't know why he's touching me. Pulling me. Where's TJ? Where's the rest of my team—

Someone yanks me backward, and I raise my gun to fire. The weapon is jerked out of my hand before I can pull the trigger, and I'm yanked toward a different bald man.

"*Soldier*, pull yourself together," he growls.

I blink.

Once.

Twice.

Then the ringing stops. Everything's burning around me until it isn't.

The sand disappears from my vision. There are no more trees or vines, or the smell of flames. Instead, there are sirens. Why are there sirens? Who is—

I gulp down air into my burning lungs and slowly glance back to the sounds of sobbing. Dinner. The private room. We were just about to leave.

Oh god.

I stagger to the person lying in the middle of the driveway. Crimson pools from his nose in a steady stream onto the concrete. *The valet assistant.* He... he can't be more than nineteen years old.

My arm gets yanked again. I whip my head around just as Sergei hisses, "We need to get out of here."

All I can do is nod. Whatever exhaustion I thought I felt before is nothing compared to the rapid beats of my pulse now. I feel like I've been strung out and the slightest pull will make me snap.

Sergei ushers Mathijs toward the SUV since the Bugatti is totaled. Mathijs holds firm, offering me his hand that I can't bring myself to take. I'm afraid that any touch is going to set me off, and asking me to *snap out of it* won't be enough.

The world shrinks until there's nothing but me, the black

SUV before me, and my memories. I don't notice the people around me or the noises. Flashes of that day hit me all over again, getting stronger the closer I get to the convoy, and everything breaks loose when my fingers wrap around the handle of the car.

The crackle of fire and tearing metal rips through my mind. The smell of smoke burns my nostrils. My ears ring. My head spins. Pain gouges a path up my legs.

It's so bright.

I can see all their bodies.

They're gone. They're all fucking dead—

We're going to get attacked. They're going to hurt TJ. I have to stop them. I—

My knees buckle, but something holds me up before I make it to the ground. I swing around to shove them against the door. My forearm presses into their throat. Yelling ensues around me, some distant sound that doesn't reach me until I start to feel something warm caressing my cheek, melting the red sheen over my vision until I can see the head of bright blond hair and deep green eyes.

So familiar. But so foreign.

I don't know where I am. What's happening? Why is he stopping me? Is he going to hurt me?

Even though I'm seconds away from hurting him, he smiles, cupping my cheek. "Come back to me," he whispers softly.

Worry lines his eyes, but the curve of his lips holds firm like we weren't just attacked, and I wasn't seconds away from pummeling him into the car because I thought I was about to be bombed all over again.

"I'm sorry." He intertwines our fingers. "We have to get in the car."

His guilt washes over me but I don't move. Breathing hard through my nose. Wishing I was someone else. Wishing the images would stop bombarding my head.

Mathijs squeezes my hand and pulls open the door, silently urging me to go inside. I'd rather walk home. Hell, I'd rather fucking die out here than go inside.

Jesus Christ, I need to get over it. It's a normal, ordinary *car*. It isn't an armored vehicle. We aren't about to drive through a desert where we would get blown off the road. This is Colorado for fuck's sake.

"Zalak," he says with a calm that I don't feel. "We have to go before Goldchild comes back to finish the job."

From the corner of my eye, I see the men standing on guard, ready to pull me off him if I try anything stupid again. I back up and breathe hard. I wouldn't be surprised if my palms are bleeding from digging my nails into them. Unspent energy thrums in my veins, begging to be released. I need to fight someone. Run. Drink. Kill. Fucking *anything* to get rid of this gnawing ache that's spread in all directions from my sternum.

Mathijs pushes off the SUV, fixes his coat, then waves away the other guards like I'm completely harmless.

I shouldn't be here. I'm not just a liability, I'm a threat to the safety of the very person I'm meant to be guarding.

Tomorrow, I'll tell him I can't do this anymore. Because

whatever progress I thought I've made these past few months was a lie. All the raids I've done, all the shoot-outs and break-ins and surveillance, all down the drain. I'm so far from any form of healing.

I'm a fucking mess, and there's nothing that will ever fix me. This was always going to be a bad idea; I was just stupid enough to believe life would become kinder.

For now, I just need to get in the goddamn car.

I squeeze my eyes shut and slide into the car. The door slams behind me and I flinch.

Shivers wrack through my body and bile clogs my throat. My gaze fixes on the window while Mathijs goes from call to call. Yelling at people and demanding information. I'm not sure why he's certain it was Goldchild when there are other threats out there. I don't have it in me to ask. If I open my mouth, I'm scared nothing is going to come out. Just like when I tried screaming for help after the bomb hit.

Once we reach the house, I throw the car door open and stumble out before it comes to a stop. I think Mathijs yells for me. I think Sergei tries to stop me. I'm not sure. I just need to get out of here. Far away from everyone.

My vision blurs and my pulse pounds in my head. The ground crunches beneath me as I run to my house.

Not *my* house. His. There's nothing that belongs to me.

Life was meant to be shaping up for me. Everything is *right there* for me to improve and stop living in the past. The raids I've done in the past two months went by fine because I was *expecting* to get shot at. How the fuck am I expected to be a guard when I can't tolerate a surprise attack?

Useless. That's what my mother would call me. *Pathetic. Good for nothing.*

I stumble into the pool house and rush for the bathroom. I hunch over the sink in an attempt to drag oxygen into my lungs. My eyes burn with unshed tears. Mom was fucking right.

What was I thinking when I got into this dress and put make-up on? Who was I trying to fool? My insides are uglier than my outsides. I need it to match. I'm meant to be scared, damaged and broken everywhere.

My fist flies out, colliding with a solid surface. The mirror shatters against my knuckles and I sob without tears. My hands keep moving. Striking out. Hoping that I might feel something other than emptiness and rage. It doesn't matter how many shards of glass embed itself into my skin, or how much crimson drips from the mirror and stains my reflection. The strikes do nothing. Why can't I fucking feel it?

I'm a mess who's better off dead. No one but Mathijs is going to mourn my passing. A week from now, everyone would have forgotten I ever existed. I'd be another number on a never-ending tally of people who never made it back from deployment.

I might have killed Mathijs. I *could* kill him one day. I was meant to be my team's eyes and I didn't see the attack coming back then. How am I meant to be someone's protector? Is this how I expect to live every day?

My mother was right. I was never meant for greatness. There

would never be a version of me where I would leave better than how I came in. All but one person I care about has died. I'm the common denominator here.

I pull my arm back and punch the mirror with a cry. It hurts somewhere deep in my center and I need to gouge it out. I stumble back, clawing at my chest to make the pain stop. My sights land on a shard of glass. Pointed like a... like a knife.

My fingers tremble as I reach for it. Blood drips down from my knuckles to the broken glass and drops to the floor. The harsh edges dig into my palms, slicing through thick skin to bring a pool of red to the surface.

I catch a glimpse of myself in the reflection, and a single word comes to mind: *Pretty*.

That's the word that crossed my mind when I saw these clothes earlier today. The person in the mirror doesn't deserve to hold any acquaintance with those two syllables after the hell that has followed me on my heels and consumed everything that's good.

I press the tip of the glass against my wrist. Crimson beads on the surface in settled silence. The slightest prick, and my nerves settle. It's the same feeling I get before I step into a ring without promise that I'll make it out alive. I push harder, hungry to fall into the headiness of acceptance. One cut, and it'll all be over. It's easier this way. Better. If I'm dead, the hurt will stop, right? I'll be with TJ and Gaya and nothing else would matter.

If the blade goes deeper, would I be met by total darkness? Would everything cease to exist? Or would I close my eyes and wake in a different body to do everything all over again just like Mom believed? Or would there be pearly gates?

"What are you doing?"

I gasp when the makeshift blade flies out of my hand and shatters on the floor. Warm arms engulf me in a tight embrace, then haul me out of the bathroom. I thrash against the hold without using any skill or tact, throwing my arms out and hoping I meet skin.

"Zalak."

No, no, no, he wasn't meant to see this. I thrash harder, but he only holds on tighter. A sob tears through my body. The carpet burns my skin as I kick my legs out fruitlessly. "Let me go," I cry.

The pain had stopped. It was getting quiet. Why did he have to ruin it? I could have finally been free and died being my mother's greatest disappointment. I left him once; he'll survive if I do it again. He knows the drill already. Sergei can protect him better than I ever could. One day I might kill him, and that would destroy me.

"Never." Mathijs lowers us to the floor, uncaring of my protests. He looks like a man who's been broken too many times and this is his last straw. Teardrops gather on the lashes surrounding his eyes that are so full of pain. It's a stark contrast to the grinning man I knew.

"Please," I beg. "You have to. I can't do it anymore. It's too late. I can't go back." *Just let me die. Please*.

He threads his fingers into my hair and presses his lips to the top of my head. "I can't lose you," he rasps.

171

Can anyone really keep a ghost? This was bound to happen eventually. I'm a ticking time bomb; it's only a matter of time when I go off.

"Let me *go*," I beg even though I've latched myself onto his clothes.

A tremor works through my voice because I... I actually don't know if I want to go. I'm just so tired of living like I'm not meant to be alive. These past few months have been so good, and every day was getting slightly better. One step forward and two steps back. That's always how it goes.

"I'm never going to let you go. I told myself that I wouldn't attend another funeral this decade. Please don't make me break that promise." His anguished voice cuts me deeper than the glass did, and the first tear drops. It trickles down my cheek and soaks into his clothes. Then more fall.

How long has it been since I cried? I don't think I did at Gaya's or my team's funerals. It was like a switch happened when the bomb went off. Why would Mathijs want someone like that? He needs someone strong and resilient. I'm a weak link. A killer lying in wake.

I shove him away, yet his hands remain on my self-inflicted wound, staunching the bleeding. "You missed me, right?" I growl. "This is what you wanted? I'm ruined, Mathijs. I'm broken beyond fucking repair. This is what you missed. This is all I'll ever be. I wasn't happy before I left this place. I wasn't happy once I was gone. I don't even know the meaning of that goddamn word. Now they're all dead and I never got the chance to say goodbye."

Tears spill into my mouth as I speak. With each word, the ache in my chest amplifies. Beneath it all is one emotion I recognize but haven't truly grasped since they died: *grief*.

They're gone and there's nothing I can do about it. They're gone and this is the first time I've spoken about them.

"You don't know what I've been through." I want to say more, but I don't know how to form the words. I'm drowning in self-pity enough as it is.

"You think I don't know what it feels like to lose everyone I've ever loved?" His voice is raw, teetering over the edge of vulnerability. "You want to end it? I get it. There hasn't been a single person in my life since my parents died. What you lived for two years, I lived for six."

Pain slices a path up my throat. "I opened my eyes, only to find that I'm the only one in my team who woke up. Then, in the same breath, they told me my entire family died due to engine failure—I didn't even know she was going to see them. If I hadn't been busy trying to prove myself, maybe she'd still be alive. If I were better at my job, maybe we could have avoided the attack," I ramble, then snap my mouth shut.

Woe is fucking me. He's telling me about his pain and I'm making this about me. How selfish and conceited could I be?

Still, he looks at me like he's absorbing every word into his marrow. He pulls me closer, shrouding me in his shuddering breaths. "None of those things are your fault." A tormented look flashes behind his eyes when he takes in the open wounds along my knuckles and palms. "I kept thinking you'd come back. And you did. But you never came to me. Not a single call. Not a text. Every single morning when I wake up, I feel sick to my stomach while I check my phone to see if you've died. And every night, I torture myself thinking that the next time I see you will be when you're in a casket."

My heart sinks into the floor, trapped under the weight of guilt. I didn't even reach out to him when his parents died because I thought he would have been better without me. Like Mom said, *Someone like him could never actually want you.* Yet here he is, not wanting to let go when he should.

I drop my gaze to his hands, and the blood trickling from the one holding on to my wrists. He tightens his grip in my hair like he senses that I'm about to move away from him.

"This isn't a competition. This isn't about the sacrifices you made. This is me saying that you aren't alone. You never were, Zalak."

I shake my head, desperate anger bubbling through me. "I'm not good for you. I never was and I never will be. Why the hell won't you get that? I'm not the seventeen-year-old girl you knew. I'm fucked in the head with no way to fix it. We can't even be in the same car as each other. You can't fly. If it weren't for me, you'd be—"

"Dead. I'd be dead."

My eyes snap up to his.

"I'm selfish. No one has been around to pick up my broken pieces until you came along."

No. I refuse to believe that. "I've done nothing for you, Mathijs."

"The only highlight of my day has been spending time with you. Just because I don't need coddling doesn't mean I don't need attention. I'm as human as you are, and the only reason I'm still standing is because I felt like I didn't have a choice. I want to make my parents proud and I knew you would come back one day—hoped for it, at least."

I squeeze my eyes shut, willing the world to disappear for just a second. But the next thing he says has me staring into his green orbs and falling deeper into his hold.

"I want you to myself, in any shape you come in, because I'll love you regardless of it. Jagged edges and all."

I choke on a sob and wrap my free arm around him, not caring where all the blood is going. Mathijs's voice curls around me like a cocoon. He grazes the line of my jaw, down to my arm where he grabs my waist to pull me onto his lap. I don't have the energy to fight it, and I don't think I want to.

"I don't think... I'm not okay, Mathijs." I curl my hands into fists to focus on my aching knuckles. "It doesn't—I don't know how I'm meant to do it—I can't *fix* it. I don't know how to. And you'd be better off..."

He nods as if he knows exactly what I'm about to say but disagrees wholeheartedly, and I couldn't be more relieved. I'm so tired of having nothing but my own company. He's been there for me these past few months, but I just couldn't accept him.

"You don't need to be alone to find yourself. Loving someone is being there to help them if they get lost along the way. It's about growing together and becoming two different puzzles that create a similar picture." Mathijs grasps my chin to tip my head up to his. "If you go, there would be nothing left inside me. So stay, Zalak. Fight me. Hate me. Do whatever you need to do to make yourself feel better. But don't leave."

What would be left of me if I walked out of here? I tried doing it all by myself, but it didn't work. I just... I needed a friend. And I've never been good at making those. If I hurt him again, I'm leaving and I'm never turning back.

I nod.

A sad smile crosses his lips—the type that says we won the battle, but not the war.

"I want you to move into the main house."

I swallow and glance at all my injuries. "You think I can't be trusted by myself? I survived this long already."

"Did you survive? Or did you die that day, and you've been walking around without your soul? Or did you lose it years before when you left home carrying nothing but your mother's words?"

I'm not sure what hurts more; his questions or the fact that I don't have the answer to them.

"Okay," I whisper.

CHAPTER 13

MATHIJS

I watch Zalak from my periphery. She's barely more than a vague lump on the roof. From here, the rifle looks like a stick poking out from the side of the building.

It's been six months since the incident in the bathroom. Six months since we've touched each other beyond a friendly embrace. Six months of watching her get back into routine—this time with fewer hours and weekly therapy sessions. It's what should have happened to begin with, but I was too optimistic. I wanted too much of her, and I didn't step back to think it through.

Every night, the last thing I see before I fall asleep is how she looked on the bathroom floor. Broken, battered, and bloody. If I had lost her, I would be done for. The fire she relit inside of me would've been permanently snuffed out. I'd continue to breathe, but I'd know the answer if she asked me the same questions—I would be soulless.

Zalak is making improvements, though—even if she often spends more time being frustrated with her so-called helplessness than anything else. She's voiced her concerns to me numerous times about how she might or might not be suited for certain missions, and that she shouldn't be kept around just to be a "charity case." For the most part, I disagreed with her assessment on her suitability for certain jobs. To begin with, at least.

There were tasks she was perfectly equipped for, except she was too caught up in doubting herself to see it. As the months progressed, her assessments became more appropriate, and Sergei was always there to monitor her and ensure that whatever we were getting into would be fine for her.

My theory is to introduce her to trigger situations at a distance so she can slowly gain control over her reactions. I spend every spare moment I have with her. She's been my plus-one to every event that has required one. A task like today's is standard, with low risk of outside influence. I wouldn't normally need a sniper when meeting someone on my payroll. But special circumstances call for special measures.

Plus, she might get to shoot someone. That sometimes puts her in a good mood.

"The new shipment of ten was dropped off to the launder. Fifteen thousand from last month's batch has been washed already," Albert says in Dutch.

The trembling fool retucks his hands into his pockets for the fourth time in two minutes. I can't believe that Goldchild trusted the idiot to play both sides. He couldn't lie to a child.

"Fifteen?" I cock a brow. "Gwendoline usually returns thirty to me in a month."

That's not entirely true. She's been dropping between one to five thousand every month over the past year. My recent visit to her confirms that she's still keeping her promise of her "dirty thirties" to me. Then she waved a gun in my face—much to Zalak's alarm—smiled, and said she can be reached by Skype if I have any follow-up questions.

Gwendoline has been washing our cash since my grandfather's time. The arrangement is that we are her only clients, and she gets a percentage of the thirty grand she washes. Being the primary cash-handler at the department store she runs has its benefits.

Albert shifts his weight. Sweat beads along his brow line even though it's meant to be a record cold month. "Changing times," he explains. "People use cash less, you know? The Feds are cracking down too. She's just being cautious."

"Is that so?"

He swallows. "Spoke to her myself. She, uh... she's thinking about retiring too. Said it's time to slow down."

I nod slowly. "She told me a different story."

"Oh yeah?" His breath audibly hitches.

Did he truly think that he could cut me short and I wouldn't find out? He'd give Gwendoline twenty thousand of my counterfeits, then throw in ten thousand of Goldchild's to keep meeting the 30k arrangement.

Not only is Goldchild on *my* territory, he's using *my* resources. I simply cannot stand for that. Picking off my men was bad enough. Using my contractors too?

Drawing a letter from my pocket, I hand it to him and take five steps back to protect my coat. Gingerly, he gives me a sideways glance before opening it. He clears his throat before he unfolds the paper, and there in black, bold letters are three words.

FUCK YOU, CUNT.

He only manages to widen his eyes before he's ripped off his feet and on his back from the force of the blow. Blood splatters on the tin walls of the warehouse, and a couple droplets make it to the hem of my pants.

I scowl. That was *cashmere.*

Closing the distance, I peer over at him, watching him gape as he touches his bleeding shoulder. "I was... I—" Albert stutters.

I sigh and look in Zalak's direction. "Second time lucky?"

Her groan crackles through my hidden earpiece.

After a couple seconds, another shot rings out. This time, the blood splatter makes it all the way up to my trench coat, and I shake my head. Well, this is going straight to the dry cleaners. The upside of the stain is that Albert has stopped being so irritating. He was a bad employee, and even worse company. *This* is my real charity.

I kick his side.

Nothing.

Splendid.

I lower myself onto my knees. Appraising the gaping hole in the center of his chest, I feel for his pulse then grin. "A confirmed kill at fifteen hundred meters."

"One thousand four hundred and fifty-two," she corrects.

"I'm rounding up."

"Two shots. It doesn't count."

"Bureaucracy is boring." Hence why I have been encouraging the use of live targets. Dummies are outdated.

"Get in the car, Mathijs."

I sigh and begin walking to the car. I love it when she gets bossy. "I hope you're in the mood for Thai tonight."

She makes a noncommittal sound.

I'll take that as a yes.

Zalak and I agreed that it's time for her to get back to working full-time. It's her second week back, and so far, there have been no incidents. I mean, it was all in good time really. Some of Goldchild's men started shooting at me while I was walking back to my car, and she only froze for a moment, then shot a guy down and remained unfazed for the rest of the night. I gave her therapist a bonus for that alone.

Goldchild—*the motherfucker*—has become even more of a nuisance. He put a hit on my head—not that Zalak knows—and it's become awfully inconvenient. Honestly, I'm quite offended that he's only offering fifty grand for my death.

Not to toot my own horn or anything, but I'd say that at an absolute *minimum* I'm worth two hundred grand.

Leaving Albert's body behind for the police or Goldchild to find, I slide into my seat and wait until I hear her motorbike rumble to life before I give the driver the signal to head home.

There's a certain peace that comes with knowing that Zalak is sharing the same roof as me. Obviously, she protested when I situated her a couple doors down from my room, but she hasn't raised an issue with it since. It makes falling asleep easier. More specifically, it makes checking on her easier—not that she knows that either.

Once I arrive home, I head straight toward the kitchen to prepare dinner. The sound of an approaching motorbike reaches me ten minutes later. Ever the overzealous guard, she must have done the rounds, tailed us to make sure we weren't being followed, then did the rounds again. I used to worry for Zalak when she was by herself. Now I worry for the people around her. Who would have guessed that killing people could be so therapeutic?

She enters the kitchen a couple minutes later and heads straight for the stereo to turn on the music. Then she picks up a knife and starts chopping the scallions. We direct each other on various tasks that require doing while she simultaneously rolls her eyes at me every time I flirt with her. It's a symbiotic relationship of sorts.

I place a hand on her waist, feeling her rock-solid muscles, then look over her shoulder as she slices the vegetables. "The way you grip that knife does things to a man, *Lieverd*."

"I will cut you with it," she says with a deadly smile.

Romance.

I grin, singing along to the music while we serve up dinner. I crack open Mom's specialty wine and pour us each a glass. We settle on the stools next to the bench and dig in. If I had to give the food a rating, I'd say six out of ten—work in progress on both our parts. The company makes up for it.

When we're finished, I turn to face her. Our next discussion has no room for uncertainty or games. It's a matter of life, death, and the future, and I need her to make her decision with her eyes wide open. Because I've already made mine.

"We need to talk." Strong start, but there's no point beating around the bush.

Zalak's brows knit, and she pushes her plate away. "Okay..."

I clasp my hands together to stop myself from reaching for her. "I am going to ask you several questions, and I want you to answer truthfully without concern for our arrangement or my feelings."

She nods slowly.

"I've told you about the secret society I'm part of. What I left out is how fucked up they are. The Reckoning is coming. Every ten years, the Exodus hosts a celebration that allows members to do whatever they wish without fear of the law. The tenth year is tomorrow." The muscle in my jaw feathers at the thought.

The first time I went continues to live in my mind like a constant reminder of all the ways this world consists of black and gray.

She frowns skeptically. "That must be why Sergei has been even more of a dick lately. Why have I never heard of any of this before? It isn't on the news. Never whispered about. Nothing."

"We control everything," I explain, as if that's sufficient enough of an answer to cover the level of corruption this country runs on.

"Why are you telling me this? Are you planning on... partaking?"

"No, no. Me? *Please*. I can do that any day of the week. I don't need a party for it." I chuckle. "There's a house within the mountains where a party will be hosted. As an Elder, my attendance is mandatory. I am required to bring a guest to the event—not to be confused with *date*, because a date would imply that you would come out unscathed. That's why we need to talk."

I told her I'd have her however she'd come. I've told her I'd wait a lifetime for her. I'd be patient, giving her everything she might need. But I want her more than anything else in this tedious world.

It kills me to just be *friends* with her. I want her in my bed every single night so the nights are less cold, then I want to wake up beside her so I know she's still with me. One day, I'll get to kiss her whenever I see her. Touch her every chance I get. I want it all, but I need her to want it too.

I wouldn't bring her to the Reckoning if I weren't so desperate for the permanence of her presence. The things that will happen there aren't for the weak. As strong as Zalak is, she might not be able to stomach the abominable things that will occur in those mountains. I barely can.

Men turn humans into toys for their deplorable entertainment. There's no elegance or decorum to how they handle themselves. It's pure debauchery without reason. Gore without the finesse. For a single night, apex predators know what it feels like to be a god. And I want to bring my girl into the fold.

"Before you answer, there are things you need to know." Christ, I should have drunk more wine. "If you say no, I will pluck one of Goldchild's men off the street and make him my party favor. If you say yes, you will be forever connected to the Exodus. You will never escape it. You will be presenting yourself as my willing guest. Forever. Do you understand what I am telling you?"

Zalak's brown eyes search mine. I wish I could tell what she's thinking. I'm prepared for her to say no because she isn't ready or because it's too soon. I doubt the cause for her hesitation has anything to do with the potential for depravity.

The skin of her knuckles goes white as she grips the stem of the wineglass. "If it's tomorrow, why are you only asking me this now?"

"Because I think you're ready for the question to be asked. You aren't the person you were when you first started working. You've become a force to be reckoned with, and I have no reservations that you'll surpass anything put before you."

Zalak has come so far in the past six months. She's still as

185

bitter as she was when we were kids, but she smiles now, and I hear her laugh almost every day. The haunted look is finally gone from her eyes, and she doesn't always have one foot in Senegal anymore.

I would have given her months to mentally prepare for tomorrow if I thought I could proposition her without worrying she'll hightail it the first chance she gets. "You will be pledging yourself to me in every sense of the word. In turn, you will be under my protection for the rest of your life. An act against you, is a direct act against everything Halenbeek. Once we take off for Vail, you won't have the opportunity to back out. So, I ask, would you like to be my plus-one and lose faith in humanity in the process?"

She hesitates. "I have no intention of leaving. I..." The *you* in her declaration is unspoken, but I hear it all the same.

At least the *humanity* part isn't her concern.

"Don't think for a second that you owe me anything," I say. "You have saved my life countless times already. That alone is priceless."

"You've saved mine just as many times. But that's not what I was going to say," Zalak says hesitantly.

Slowly, *ever so slowly*, she places her hand next to mine, touching me without my prompting it. My breath catches in my throat when she finally interlocks our fingers. Willingly. Voluntarily. Then it's knocked right out of my lungs when she looks at me with the same reverent need that I feel for her.

She squeezes my hand. "I don't want to live in the past anymore, Mathijs."

This woman couldn't get any more perfect even if she tried. A smile explodes across my face, and I raise my wineglass. "To the future."

And to the fuckery that will ensue tomorrow.

CHAPTER 14

ZALAK

W hat am I about to get myself into?

Secret societies? A day of complete lawlessness? This all sounds well over my pay grade. It isn't too late for me to back out. Hell, I even helped catch the guy who'd be my substitute in case I decide to tap out.

Still, I stare at my reflection in the mirror. I've outdone myself this time. The déjà vu is unsettling.

There was another outfit waiting for me on my bed once I got to my room. This time, it's a crimson *lehenga* with intricate gold beading and a cream bikini blouse. It's paired with a matching filigree necklace, earrings, and bangles. All my tattoos are on show again, only this time I have full range of upper body movement, and I can wear a pair of shorts underneath.

After almost eight months working here, Mathijs has finally understood that I prefer form over fashion—though it'll be difficult to run or climb anything in this skirt.

Swallowing a sigh, I slip into my coat and then head downstairs where Mathijs is talking to Sergei beside a golf cart.

My stomach twists that they both know what my kryptonite is, and we've resorted to carting around like children. I've tried getting over it countless times over the past month to no avail. Instead, I've managed to recognize exactly what my triggers are, which means that limos and sports cars are still on the agenda—it's a very expensive coping mechanism.

Mathijs rakes his gaze over me with enough heat that I might as well be naked. He's the most stunning man I've ever met, inside and out. Every time I'm around him, I feel seen in a way that I struggle to describe. He's stuck around despite seeing all my bad parts, and I've come to realize that it's not something I ever want to lose. Wherever he goes, I'm going to follow. There's no doubt about it in my mind.

He needs me just as much as I need him. I see it now.

Excitement flashes in his eyes. "Ready, *Lieverd*?"

I scoff nervously. "Are you?"

"Absolutely fucking not."

Oh great.

I give him a rueful smile while Sergei climbs behind the wheel of the cart. "It sounds like you might be catching a cold," I say, giving him a pathetic excuse to get out of tonight. "I'd hate for you to pass it around to your buddies."

"If only the flu would kill some of them," Mathijs mutters, then holds me hostage with his stare, silently communicating that the choice is still in my hands.

My throat bobs. "I understand the implications and I want to go."

Lie. I'm not sure I'm fully aware of what I'm signing up for. But I know that whatever it is, it means that I'm committing myself to this type of life.

He holds out his hand, and I take it without a hesitation. The mindless gesture has him smiling from ear to ear as if we aren't about to walk into hell, and he's just a kid getting to hold his crush's hand. He helps me into the cart like the gentleman he is. Then Sergei starts the little engine before speeding through the property to get to the hangar.

"Chances are that Goldchild knows about tonight. He could see it as an opening to attack our factories. I want double patrols and all hands on deck. Put the men who are meant to travel with us on watch duty at the compound—including you, Sergei," Mathijs says.

Excuse me?

The head of security and I both jerk toward Mathijs.

"That'll leave you exposed," I argue.

Sergei grunts in agreement.

"I'll have you there," Mathijs says to me.

"As a *guest*." I motion to my clothes. "I'm hardly dressed for a fight, and you told me that no weapons are allowed."

His eyes drop to the backpack containing the sniper that I

brought with me. "There will be security on site, and I need Sergei here if things go south. Goldchild wouldn't be stupid enough to attack the event."

I grind my teeth, and I swear the Russian does the same, saying, "We can spare two men to fly with you."

"Two men, or you won't make it on the helicopter in one piece," I threaten. None of us have seen the layout of the perimeter or have complete information on the level of security at this place. There are simply too many risks and moving variables that are worse with the lack of information.

"Don't threaten me with a good time." He smirks. "When you say it like that, I don't have a choice but to agree."

Sergei grabs his phone and fires off orders to whoever is on the other line. I jolt in my seat when Mathijs's hand lands on my knee. His only explanation for the move is a wink. Warmth spreads through my touch-starved body, and I fix my gaze forward since we have an audience. He's gradually becoming bolder with his touches, and it drives me absolutely wild because I just want him to hold me and smother me with affection, but I can't find it in me to ask.

Once we arrive at the hangar, Mathijs takes the seat in the cockpit, and an actual pilot sits beside him to play copilot. The discussion regarding security measures and strategy doesn't end when we're in the helicopter and no longer on land. The two men sent with us are senior enough that they actually bring something useful to the conversation we're having. But they mainly stay silent while Mathijs and I talk about Goldchild.

Goldchild is getting restless, which means he's becoming more ruthless in his approach. This morning, he took out one of our washers. We thought the plan might have been to take out the boss and swallow Mathijs's operation, but it's become clear that the plan is to burn the whole organization to the ground with everyone inside.

All cards are off the table now, and we all have free rein on Goldchild's men, or as Mathijs calls them: target practice.

The flight takes less than an hour, and by the end of it, he looks half tempted to turn around and risk the society's wrath instead. It's not exactly a look that fills me with much confidence. The trees bow away from the helicopter and the leaves shake as we descend, and I jolt when we touch the ground.

Much to Mathijs's disapproval, I help myself out and unbutton my coat as a fine layer of sweat builds down my spine from the eerily warm night. Moonlight glints off the machine behind me. As the rotors slow, music filter between the trees, and the distinct sound of laughter and... crying. My eyes dart across the forest, keeping my ears peeled for bird songs or insects, but there's nothing but the sound of distant wailing.

I glance back at Mathijs's approach to gauge if I'm just imagining it. He seems unsurprised by the ominous tone. Even the two men and the pilot who joined us are unfazed by it.

Swell. We might all die tonight.

A shiver works its way through my bones, and I stamp it down. It is too late to back down now.

"Not to alarm you," Mathijs starts, well and truly alarming

me, "but I'm going to need you to wear this."

He holds up what looks like a black tie, and I take a step back. Any reservations I have about this event doubles. I don't want to back out of this, but I also don't want to go in blind. "Why?"

A haunted look passes over his features. "Whatever you think you saw when you were deployed... the real monsters are at home. Put the mask on. *Please.*"

The regretful burning in his eyes is the only reason I don't go up in arms over the request. With a deep breath, I nod. He doesn't relax at my acceptance, but still, he wastes no time in tying the blindfold over my eyes, plunging the world around me into total darkness.The cold sticks to my clammy skin as I try to get my bearings. I trust Mathijs implicitly for all matters that don't involve his own personal security. The things I do for this man.

"Wait in front of the house," Mathijs orders the two guards before placing his hand on my lower back and intertwining our fingers with his other, steering me through the forest.

My lungs constrict at the loss of sight, suffocating and sharpening me at the same time. All my other senses heighten with my rising adrenaline. The sounds of the party seem closer, and the crisp air burns through my nostrils, making me notice things I wouldn't have otherwise. Trust in Mathijs isn't enough to stop my steps from being uncertain and slow—whether it's from reluctance or understandable cautiousness, it would be complete idiocy to walk into this mess with full confidence.

As we near, another sound reaches my ears that I didn't hear before.

I still. "Why are people moaning, Mathijs?"

His harsh breath brushes through my hair, and I shiver. "Pleasure and pain go hand in hand."

I whip my head toward him even though I can't see a thing. "What is that supposed to mean?" More importantly, does that involve *me*?

"We won't be taking part in those festivities."

I tense. "Do we need to take part in *something*?"

"Yes."

I shove his hands off me and rip off the blindfold. If I'm partaking in whatever the fuck is going on in there, he should have told me beforehand. "Enough of this cryptic crap. You better start talking right now, or so help me god, Mathijs."

He shifts his weight. "You have two options: join or be sacrificed."

"Excuse me?"

"You can either choose to carry out the task I set for you so you can prove that you are worthy of being associated with us, or you will die."

What type of fucked-up bullshit has he dragged me into? Have I not *proven* myself to these people by keeping Mathijs alive? Did I not kill enough men for these goddamn people?

"Why did you invite me to this, Mathijs?"

"Because I want you in my life, and this is how it's done. You need to prove you belong by my side, or else they'll consider you a weak link."

I swipe my hand over my face and count to ten. "How?"

He takes a deep breath. "You've proven it to me before. It's nothing you aren't capable of."

More obscure answers. I take a deep breath and weigh my options. Mathijs wouldn't have kept me alive and spent so much time with me if he expected me to become *sacrificed* by the end of it. He'll do right by me. Whatever that might mean. And I'm willing to do what it takes for the sake of our relationship, and proving to him just how committed I am without actually saying the words.

I make my peace with death every time I wake up and step into potential lines of fire. The only difference this time is that it feels like my fate is in his hands, more than it is in mine.

I hesitate before tying the fabric around my eyes again. I'd risk it all for him. That hasn't changed. If that needs to be further proven, then so be it. He's been patient with me while I found my footing again, and I know how I want my future to look.

The air between us is tenser than before, and the slightest hint of something metallic hits the back of my throat. *Blood*.

Men's laughter sounds in the distance, followed by more guttural screams that send my nerves into a frenzy. Each noise becomes more distinct the closer we get to the house.

We come to a sudden stop. I hear one of our men behind me pass something to Mathijs. I can make out the sound of a dial spinning right before a set of latches open. Then there's rustling and a slight grunt. I'm tempted to remove my blindfold again, but something tells me that I don't want to risk knowing what's happening. Blissful ignorance sounds more like a dream right now.

Mathijs goes back to guiding me up the slope. The ground shifts from wet earth, to grass, to concrete, and the sounds become clear as day. What I thought might have been one or two people moaning or crying out in pain, sounds like a whole group. A bloodcurdling scream pierces the still night air, and I narrowly manage to stop myself from staggering back.

Mathijs urges me forward, and I get the hint: *don't show weakness.*

He helps me up a couple steps, and we reach what must be a security guard standing in front of the entrance because I can just see the tips of their shoes at the bottom of my blindfold.

Two guards at the front, I tally.

Something beeps and the security steps aside to let us in. All the sounds hit me at once, and it's a physical feat not to cringe away from it. The place smells like carnage and sex. It clogs my throat and a wave of nausea goes through me. I have a feeling the military couldn't have prepared me for what comes next.

Mathijs ushers me along. All I can see is a sliver of the floor beneath me, shifting from wooden floors to carpet, or a vintage rug. I mentally note how many steps we take before turning left or right. He leads me down a flight of stairs into a basement where the roar of a crowd bounces along the walls. People cheer, yell, boo, and everything in between. Familiarity prickles my skin, raising the hairs on the back of my neck. It sounds like...

Mathijs undoes the tie once we reach the bottom step, revealing the mayhem in front of me. My lips part. It isn't a basement; it's a bunker. It has a high ceiling, concrete walls, and hanging lights that are still despite the chaos of the room.

This is a fighting ring.

I turn to Mathijs, but a stag's skull stares back at me—more specifically, an *edelhert*. Its horns are dipped in gold, and there's a golden sheen over the bone. Every person in here is wearing a mask of some sort in either black or white. Only Mathijs's has any gold on it.

There are more black masks among the crowd, but each one is slightly different. A man passes me wearing a white head of a dragon, another wears a gas mask, and another has a balaclava on. There are several women wearing masks as well, but they're few and far between.

I spot about eight people whose faces are exposed. I can only assume that they're guests like me.

Fucking hell, how many people have been dragged here to prove something?

The crowd doubles in volume and my attention snags on the raised platform in the middle of the room. One man has the other in a headlock, then an audible *snap* that echoes through the room. Then the body falls limp.

Screaming and shouting ensues. The bloodlust in the air is palpable, turning my stomach inside out. It's been far too long since I've been to something like this.

Mathijs's hand remains firm at the small of my back. Foot-steps behind us make me turn, ready to step in front of him, but

I stop short when another man wearing a golden mask appears before us.

The man tips his head down at Mathijs who returns the gesture. A silent understanding goes between them that I can't translate. Then he glances at me for a second too long before walking back up the stairs like nothing happened.

"You want to know what your task is?"

My head snaps up to meet Mathijs. His eerie mask makes it impossible to read how he's feeling.

A battle cry sounds from the middle of the room.

He wants me to fight.

I swallow. "When?"

He trails his finger along my cheek.

Mathijs solidified my strength these past months—both physically and mentally since I haven't felt pain in my foot for so long. Even at the prospect of dying in the ring, I'd still do it all for him. *Lose it all.*

My agreement to do this isn't just for him or some society. It's a chance for me to prove to myself how far I've come from the person who only fought for the high and some cash. There's something bigger than myself, and I have every intention of being part of it.

"Once you're ready," Mathijs says in answer.

"Lead the way."

Even though I want to reach for him and seek comfort in his touch, I let him navigate us through the crowd and through a set of doors that takes us to the bottom floor. He opens the locker room for me, and I take a wary step inside. It's similar to many other underground places I've been to, only it's actually clean.

On the bench in the middle of the room is a duffle bag containing everything I might need for the fight; a mouth guard, wraps, even clothes. With a single finger, I raise the sports bra in the air.

It's simple, black, and in my size.

I glare at Mathijs and his *edelhert* mask. He planned every step of this and banked on my agreement. What would have happened if he had brought Goldchild's man instead? Would he be standing where I am, or would he be one of the screams I heard upstairs?

I don't appreciate that he didn't tell me all the information so I could go into this with my *eyes wide open*. But I understand why he kept it from me. I would have lost sleep thinking about what I was about to do, and thrown myself back into the past where I was looking forward to a fight just to get my kicks. Given the option to change his tactics, I'd ask that he does the same.

He closes the distance between us and cups my cheek. "You can get ready here. No one will bother you. I have to organize some things, and someone will get you once it's time."

His voice is a hoarse whisper, there's no doubt for what's next. He isn't holding on to me like it might be the last time he can do it. Rather, he's sending me a message with his tender touch.

"I believe in you, *Lieverd*."

I nod stiffly, but grasp his wrists like I don't want to let him go

199

even though I know I have to. We stand there for what could be hours, with me, staring up at his masked face. When he finally turns to leave, the silence becomes deafening.

Steeling my spine, I start the preparation process of changing into clothes I can move in. I bind both my hands with tape and a wrap, then begin my warm-ups.

My mind threatens to take me back to all the years I spent in places like this, but I manage to stay in the present. That was a different life with different circumstances. I have a support structure now and someone I care about, who cares for me in return. But fuck if it isn't nerve-wracking.

A knock rattles the door once half an hour passes. "They're ready."

My heart rate skyrockets. The surge of adrenaline is heady and addicting. It rings in my ears and makes my muscles coil. The anxieties I felt earlier are dull beneath the electricity thrumming in my veins.

"Give me a minute," I call out.

Tentatively, I reach for my purse and grab the dog tags and Gaya's pendant inside. The gold coin is cool against my lips, and for a second, I let myself imagine that she's still here, sitting at home waiting for me to return. With a fleeting glance at my dog tags, I place them both back in the bag and hide it in one of the lockers.

I catch myself in the reflection and almost don't recognize myself like this. Every other time I've looked in a grimy mirror in an abandoned parking lot or warehouse, I hated what I saw.

An emotion bubbles in my chest—something akin to pride. There's meat and muscle on my bones, color in my skin, and light in my eyes.

I bite into the mouth guard, then rip the door open. A man with a black mask leans against the concrete wall, waiting for me. The buzzing in the air adds to the energy pulsing through me as we reach the main room.

I'm going to kill a man tonight.

I might even smile while I do it.

I'll break bones and spill my own blood. Still, only one of us is walking out alive.

My mother wanted a son, but she got something far worse.

Me.

The door opens and the roar of the crowd slams into me, making me soar three feet higher. Mathijs steps onto the platform and holds up a hand. In an instant, the room descends into silence.

I stay standing in front of the door, studying the crowd. On the opposite side of the room is a man I recognized from earlier. One of the guests. He has to be over six foot three, all arms and legs with lean muscles. Our eyes clash as we size each other up.

"Two more of our guests will enter this ring tonight. One will live," Mathijs's voice booms through the bunker. "Prey becomes predator, and the only gift is their life. Only the strongest survive within the Exodus, and survival is our biological incentive." I can picture him grinning beneath his mask, basking in all the attention. "But is it not the day of the Reckoning? Do we not want a show?"

People whistle and yell their agreement, and the anticipation of the crowd builds to near boiling.

"As a token of my appreciation for the caliber of guests you have all brought tonight, the winner will receive a four-hundred-thousand-dollar prize."

Goosebumps rain over my flesh and I stare daggers into my boss. How much more shit is this guy keeping from me? Is *not dying* going to be enough of a prize?

Also, what the fuck am I meant to do with four hundred thousand dollars? I'm a live-in guard whose chosen mode of transport is a motorbike I practically built myself. Actually, I'll give half of it to Amy and the other half to TJ's family. They need it more than I do.

Mathijs points toward my opponent. "To my right, we have Justin MacMillan." The crowd's reaction is mediocre at best. "He's been vying for a place amongst our ranks for years. Tonight, he'll prove to us if he's worthy to be part of the Exodus."

The lackluster applause must infuse Justin with enough confidence, since he looks at me smugly then puffs his chest out and practically swaggers up to Mathijs's side. Oh, spare me a break. Countless hopeful recruits have stared me down and challenged me just because they're a head taller and I have a vagina.

Pretty boy over there hasn't seen war. I doubt he's ever killed someone before. Still, he's lithe enough to be considered a threat due to his strength and speed alone. It's only a matter of finding out whether his arrogance is founded or fuel from his ego.

Mathijs raises his hand once more to stop the few people screaming their support for the rookie.

"To my left, my guest." He pauses for dramatic effect, and everyone turns my way. "The *Deathstalker*."

There's no cheer. Not a single whistle. The silence is so deadly, I'd be able to hear a pin drop. I've had reactions like this before because most wouldn't be able to imagine a woman stepping into the ring. Let alone against another man.

I stalk forward, avoiding eye contact with anyone but Justin. Men and women part for me. Their masks stare blankly, and their whispers feather over me.

The cockiness wipes off his face the closer I get, and the line of his shoulders tighten as he takes me in. Justin finally sees me for what I am.

A threat.

CHAPTER 15

ZALAK

My head whips to the side from the force of his blow. Blood drips from my lip and nose, but really, the other guy is worse for wear. I'm surprised he can see any of the attacks I throw his way when his eyes are practically swollen shut.

I kick my leg out, winding him at the same time I throw a punch at his good eye. The crowd cheers, screaming *Death-stalker* as if the name belongs to a god. I almost grin at Justin because of how poetic the situation is.

His fanbase turned on him. Even people I saw betting on him are yelling with delight every time I land a hit.

When the underdog comes out on top, one of two things happens: people either get really happy or come searching for blood.

I launch at him while he's disoriented, laying hit after hit on him. He struggles to block a single one, bunching his shoulders and hiding behind his curled fists.

My initial observations were true. He's fast, has an endless well of stamina, and can pack a punch. But his skills start and end there. His attacks are undisciplined like he's learned how to fight by getting into one, rather than actual practice. But the asshole just won't drop.

I growl in annoyance when he buries his knee in my gut.

Catching his next punch, I yank the cockroach forward and use gravity to take him down onto the floor. I hold his torso and head down with my legs and hug his arm, pulling it back until I hear a satisfying *snap*. He cries out and clamps his teeth down on my leg like a fucking animal.

Oh, so he wants to play dirty? Fine. I'll play fucking dirty.

I yank the arm back again, forcing him to loosen his jaw enough for me to pivot and bring my elbow down on his crotch.

Panting, I clamor on top of him, only to grapple for dominance. We take turns having the upper hand, but he can only do so much harm with a dislocated elbow and crushed cock. Once I end up back on top, I waste no time laying into his face.

Like the goddamn pest he is, he manages to throw me off balance enough to stop an attack. Before he can do further damage, I'm on my back with his head between my legs, holding his good arm.

He tries bucking. Biting. Hitting. Anything humanly possible to make me loosen my hold on him. With each harsh breath that I take, the fight drains from him until he can't do more than twitch. I hold on for another twenty seconds to make sure he's out, then I push onto my feet to drop my heel into his throat with every ounce of strength. Tendons and ligaments bend and snap beneath the force.

I'm not about to choke him out for ten minutes to make sure he's dead. Breaking his windpipe is the next best option. He's as good as dead now.

I'm deaf to the roar of the crowd, but it doesn't stop me from absorbing the energy from my triumph.

Look at me, Mom. It's your favorite son.

I spit on his corpse, then stalk off the stage with a backward glance at Mathijs. I can picture him grinning like a lunatic beneath his mask, and the thought of it makes the victory of the fight sweeter.

The locker room appears exactly the same as how I left it. I help myself to the adjoining shower to wash the blood and sweat sticking to my skin, wincing when the hot water hits the open wounds on my face. It's still bleeding by the time I shut the water off and wrap the towel around myself. I curl my fingers into a tight fist and swing the door open quickly in case anyone is behind the door.

There is.

But he's no threat to me.

The stag mask is no longer on his head but on the bench against the wall.

"What are you doing here?" I ask as I move to the bag to

change into the outfit I arrived in. If it weren't for my years in the military, getting dressed in front of Mathijs might have sent me into cardiac arrest. Instead, I'm hedging the line of a fever with how weighted his gaze is.

The air between us is so thick, I doubt a bullet would be able to fly through it. I try to tell myself that it's all in my head, but the fire burning inside me knows that I'm not fooling anyone.

"You forgot to grab your prize." He smiles. Except there's no mischief or hidden meaning behind it. Even his voice is soft with an eager edge, and his eyes are bright with elation.

I grin, ignoring the pain in my cheek as I slip on my underwear and shorts beneath the towel. "I don't need your money. You can keep it, or I'll donate it to Gaya and TJ, and some other charities."

"I never said it was a cash prize."

I pause just as I'm about to put on the beaded top. "Then what is it?"

"Why don't you get dressed first?"

Narrowing my eyes, I nod. My back is to him up until the point I'm wearing everything I arrived in, there's a Band-Aid on my forehead, and my hair is braided down my back. "What is it then?" I ask, eyeing the black box in his hand.

He throws it my way, and I catch it midair. Velvet covers encase the little box that's smaller than the palm of my hand. It's a... a jewelry box?

Slowly, I click open the lid and suck in a sharp breath at the big, emerald-cut diamond staring back at me. More diamonds wrap around the golden band; it's so subtle I could have missed it. It's stunning.

I'm pretty sure Justin wouldn't have appreciated winning an engagement ring—

My eyes snap to Mathijs, and I almost gasp when I find him on one knee. "Marry me, Zalak. Make me complete."

Every fiber of my being freezes at that moment. I want to say yes. I want to scream it because it was always meant to end this way.

The other part of me is questioning how ready I am for it. I took the plunge tonight by agreeing to come here, even with all the consequences of my attendance in mind. The romantic, more intimate double meaning of my acceptance wasn't lost on me either.

Everyone here has seen my face and knows that I came here in the arms of one of their leaders. I knowingly risked my life to do it. There's no mistaking the pledge I made to him and his organization when I killed a man in cold blood.

I'm ready to risk my life for him. I walked into this blind because I wanted to prove to Mathijs just how dedicated I am to him.

So why am I stopping at a label that comes with a ring? The lack of physical intimacy we've had in six months shouldn't be a factor since it's clearly not a concern to him.

"I'm not the type of person someone falls irrevocably in love with," I say, more to give him a chance to change his mind.

"I could be six feet under, and I'd still walk the afterlife every day by your side. There's nothing about you that I would change. You're it for me, *Lieverd*."

I blink back the tears gathering along my waterline. "There should be. No one's perfect."

Yet he is.

"You're the closest thing to it. And still, I love the parts of you that aren't."

I let him take my hand and the little box. I'll never find anyone like him for as long as I live. I've never met anyone so patient. He's seen every broken piece, and still looks at me like I'm the most beautiful thing he's ever seen.

"Marry me. There will never be anyone else for me but you."

My first nod comes out uncertain. The second comes a little more confidently. There's no mistaking the enthusiasm of the third. "Yes." I choke on a sob and drop onto my knees in front of him. "Yes, yes, yes. I'll marry you."

The smile that explodes across his face makes my heart triple in size. My entire body trembles with uncontainable emotion as he slides the ring onto my finger. In the next blink, my lips are on his, and our hands are all over each other. All that's here is *him*. The feel of his hands, the smell of him, the way he kisses me back like I'm the cure he's been searching for.

My fingers claw at his shoulders like I need him to breathe. He bites my bottom lip and I moan, digging my nails into him. The arm he has around my waist is the only reason I haven't toppled over. I reach for his pants at the same time he goes for my *lehenga*.

He's ripped away from me before I manage to undo his belt. My arms fly out in front of me to catch my fall. Pain erupts across my face before I can steady myself, and I land on my side with an *oomph*.

Groaning, I pry my eyes open and cringe from the ringing in my ears. I sway as I try to raise myself up onto my elbows to make sense of what's happening. As I blink, three blurry figures come into view—I can just make out the masks covering their faces.

"Goldchild sends his regards."

A fist collides with my cheek and knocks me back onto the floor. Air tears from my lungs at the same time they kick my stomach. I buckle over and gasp for oxygen while the world around me spins. The high-pitched sound is earsplitting. I can't even hear the sound of my own cry.

It gets worse every time I try to get up. I manage to hold down the bile lurching up my throat, but still, I struggle to reorient myself.

"Mathijs," I croak.

All I can see is a flurry of white and black dots. My head swims as the ringing slowly abates. Every inch of my body screams at me to lie back down and close my eyes.

"Mathijs," I repeat.

Nothing.

I wince as I rub my eyes to get rid of the haze over my vision. I keep blinking until the orbs disappear and the room clears.

It's empty.

No.

"Mathijs," I say louder this time, scrambling up to my feet. I stumble out into the hallway, then look left and right. They took him.

CHAPTER 16

ZALAK

F uck.

Fuck, fuck, fuck.

I trip over my feet as I clamor back into the room to grab my phone from my purse. My head swims and the letters on my screen come up as double. I manage to dial Josh's number, one of the men who came with us.

"Hello," the voice crackles through the speaker.

"Goldchild took Mathijs," I pant, using the wall for support as I stumble through the corridors.

"What? Shit. Where?" Either Josh or Aiden hisses to someone beside them, "Goldchild's got Halenbeek."

I stop to pull up Mathijs's locator on my phone. I've never been so grateful that he had himself chipped like a dog in case of situations like this. I squint at the screen to figure out where the little dot is moving on the map. *Jesus Christ*. How long was I out for that they're already on the road?

"Toward Denver."

The hallway twists and turns as I tumble straight ahead in an attempt to retrace my steps out of this messed-up place. My face is throbbing. My ribs are aching. I'm so damn exhausted, and I want Mathijs back.

Okay, think, Zalak. We need a plan, and I need the fog to disperse from my goddamn brain.

"One of you grab my backpack from the helicopter. Then find us a fucking car."

"It's faster if we fly—"

"We don't know where they're taking him. And it's too loud. Get it done. I'll meet you out front in five." If I can make it out of here. If I don't, they could kill Mathijs and—

I choke on the panic, and stamp it as far down as I can. I spent ten years of my life training for this type of situation. Emotions are what gets a person killed in the line of duty. If I drop the ball, Mathijs will die. Plain and simple.

"But—"

I hang up before they can waste more of my energy. Leaning against the wall, I let myself have a twenty-second break to close my eyes, focus on my breathing, and clear my head. Nothing more. Nothing less.

Fuck. I hate going into this type of shit blind. Both figuratively, and *especially* literally.

When I reopen my eyes, much of the disorientation has dissipated, and it doesn't feel like I'm going to keel over to pass out or throw up. I manage to get myself to the set of stairs that leads into the bunker.

No one pays me any mind, and I stagger when I spot a man with a slit throat lying on the floor. A wolf whistle breaks my thoughts. I turn toward it and spot two people fucking against the wall.

I'm no closer to determining whether there's another exit out of this bunker that they dragged Mathijs through, or if they simply put a random mask on him, then walked right up these steps.

I sprint up the stairs and out into a study. I eye the sliding bookshelf behind me that's hiding the entrance to the bunker, then shake my head and run to the exit. I stay close to the wall just in case my legs give out on me. There's the same sounds as before: screaming, fucking, moaning, crying, laughter, music.

I try to recall the tally I made when I didn't have my full senses. How many steps did I take before each turn? When did the flooring change? I just need to do it in reverse.

Left, I decide when I make it to the corridor.

My pulse thunders against my skin. Through the fog, my mind keeps threatening to remind me about all the things that could happen to Mathijs. I can't lose him too. I'm not strong enough to recover from that kind of blow so soon after I managed to tape myself together.

I charge forward, paying attention to the flooring. I don't

dare look into the rooms, but the occasional blood drop on the floor is unmistakable. I pause to glance out of the window to make sure it at least appears like I'm heading in the right direction, but it's another useless tactic.

I keep going around, backtracking and taking various turns when, *finally*, I reach the main foyer. A hand lands on my shoulder just as I throw the front door open, and I whirl around to the idiot.

The *Men in Black* wannabe sneers at me like I'm trying to break out of prison. Based on what I've gleaned from this place so far, it might look that way. "Get back inside. You—"

"Have a fucking security breach."

He looks at me blankly. "You can't leave without permission from your—"

I don't have time for this bullshit.

"They fucking kidnapped Mathijs Halenbeek. So I am going to give you five more seconds to remove your hand from me before I consider you an accomplice to his kidnapping."

He shoots a questioning glance at the two other men guarding the door. "That can't be—"

I step forward. "Do I *look* like I'm joking? If he's dead, I'm going to find you and make a lanyard out of your fucking intestines. You have two more seconds. Tick tock."

One of the men grunts in silent order for me to be released. I dart out of the house as soon as I'm free and spot two of Halenbeek's men. Josh holds up my backpack, and Aiden fires up the engine of the SUV they commandeered.

Josh leaves the passenger door open and climbs into the back. I slide in and start firing off directions on where to go. The little dot on my phone keeps moving, picking up an unhealthy amount of speed. I call Sergei to debrief him on the situation—and *his*, since Goldchild chose to hit one of our warehouses.

Once we hit the highway that they're also flying through, there's nothing for me to do except watch the screen since I've assembled the sniper and we're decked out with more weapons than any person might need.

Something in the glove compartment rattles, and I stay still. My pulse stops. My lungs squeeze. My blood drops by ten degrees. Everything hits me at once: the rotation of wheels on asphalt. The hum of the motor. The wind passing the car.

The *car*.

I'm in a car.

I dig my nails into the fabric of the car.

I got in, and I didn't think twice about it.

I'm in here.

I did it.

My breathing shallows at the realization. The more I think about where I am, the more suffocated I become in this metal can. Anyone could shoot at us. There could be people hiding behind the—

"They just turned off," Josh says.

I drag my focus back to the phone I've affixed to the dashboard. *Right*. Mathijs. There's no time to think about where

I am. Sergei and his men are at least an hour out, and they're dealing with a different shitstorm. Any men that can be spared would need to arrive by helicopter, and it's not exactly the most silent mode of transport. We're the only ones who can save him right now.

I quickly pull up my contacts and call Mathijs's tech girl who I've already spoken to tonight. Maddie pulls up all the addresses in the area that they're heading in, and attempts to narrow down their location. They're sticking to the back roads which is slowing them down, but I imagine it's an attempt to get off the main roads to avoid being caught on camera.

She sends me the blueprints of the whole area they've stopped at. It's a compound. We pull up to a stop down the road from the place, far enough away that it won't raise any flags. By the time we get there, Sergei and several teams of men are twenty minutes out, which means that the three of us can't go in guns blazing without risking Mathijs's life.

We trek down the mountain, following the map Maddie sent.

A shiver works down my spine from the combination of adrenaline and the cold air. It might be unseasonably warm for this time of year, but the moisture seeping into my clothes and bare arms makes matters all the more miserable.

Of course I'm doing this shit in a big skirt and heels. And I forgot my fucking coat. Trust Mathijs to make sure I'm improperly dressed for action.

I grit my teeth and use a tree as support to steady myself as I break the heels off my expensive shoes, and rip the *lehenga* off so

217

I'm just in my shorts, then trudge through the Colorado woods. I'm going to kill him myself if we both survive this.

We collectively pause when a gunshot echoes through the forest. We snap our attention to each other, then sprint toward the compound.

The hairs at the back of my neck stand on end. I push myself harder, kicking up dirt and fallen leaves. We come to a screeching halt when we reach a twelve-foot-high fence, decked out with barbed wire and electricity.

Son of a bitch.

Cursing, I run around the perimeter until I have a view of something—*anything*. I systematically raise the sniper scope to my eyes each time there's an opening through the trees.

"You're getting further away from the—"

"Shut up," I snap before Josh can finish putting in his unwanted two cents.

We need higher ground, a view, and to get away from the cameras he so conveniently didn't notice.

A quick check of my phone shows that Sergei is five minutes out.

Mathijs has been in Goldchild's custody for well over twenty minutes. The first fifteen are the most crucial. We don't have time to sit and wait for Sergei, and since none of us can scale the fence, we need to improvise.

My gaze darts to a boulder tucked into the earth, then to the view of a property to the right. Without bothering to tell the two men to sit put, I swing the sniper around to my back and use the tree roots to climb up to the top of the stone. It's a tight fit between the dirt wall and the edge of the boulder, but it's just long enough for me to lie on my stomach and set the rifle.

I look down the scope and adjust it to carefully survey the compound to get a better grasp on what we're dealing with and if I can be of any help once Sergei arrives.

It's a typical mountain home with brick walls and plenty of chimneys. The only thing that sets it aside is the copious number of warehouses and garages scattered throughout the compound, far enough from the main home to give it some privacy.

We've never been able to narrow down where Goldchild's factory might be. This is probably where the magic happens.

Several armed men walk about the compound, rushing from one place to another, all ripe for the killing.

Aiden passes me the backpack and I make quick work of setting up the ballistic computer with the rifle for better accuracy. Another breath, and I'm back to scoping out the place.

"What do you see?" Josh asks while they both do laps around our perimeter.

I ignore him.

"Do you see—"

"Stop talking," I grate out.

My heartbeat stalls when I make it to the back of the main house. They have Mathijs chained up by his wrists, half naked, hanging from a pole that's sticking out from the side of a pavilion. Purple and blue blotches decorate his pale skin. Blood braids through his blond hair, and drips down his torso, dotting the concrete like blooming poppies.

Bile lurches up my throat but I hold it down. Cold sweat coats my skin as an older, beer-gutted man with knuckle busters throws another punch.

Red falls over my vision. My finger twitches over the trigger, and I have to move it on top of the trigger guard to stop myself from doing anything rash.

It's not a kill blow. Mathijs will survive it. If I shoot now, I'll give away our location, and they'll end his life.

Grabbing my phone from inside my top, I call Sergei. He answers on the second ring. "I have eyes on *Edelhert*. Back porch of the main house. A click from the main road. One point five clicks west of my position."

He grunts. "How many guards?"

"Twelve that I've seen. Armed."

"We're three minutes out."

Just then, the bald man torturing Mathijs turns. My lips curl into a sneer. "Goldchild's here."

"You have a shot."

I hesitate. "Affirmative."

"Wait for my signal."

The line stays on as he fires instructions to everyone else.

"Aiden, watch my six. Josh, head down to assist. You've got three minutes to get there."

I don't check if he listens, focusing on calculating the shot. The nerves wracking my body make it hard to keep a steady hand. My pulse is running rapidly, my head is pounding, and my breaths are unsteady. A rookie would have a better chance at success compared to the state I'm in.

If I fuck up, he dies. If I don't get it together, he dies. If I can't get a grip, then years of training and duty were for nothing.

Closing my eyes, I let myself imagine that TJ is next to me, silently giving me instructions and keeping me up to date on the world outside of the pinpoint I can see. When that doesn't calm my nerves, I picture him looking down on me, wherever he is, doing just the same with a beer in his hand.

"*Eh, I don't think you can make the shot, Scorp*," he'd say with a grin every time we were going long range. "*How about you give it up and let a real man have a crack at it. Thirteen hundred feet? A woman couldn't pull something like that off.*"

TJ would always goad me into things, and tease me until I wanted to beat him up, but the challenge fueled my spite, amping up my need to prove him wrong. After all, it's the same words he said to me when I made my record.

"*How about this, you shoot the fucker dead and I'll do your laundry for a week. You miss, then you do mine. I should warn you, girly. I've got some nasty ones for you to deal with.*"

His incessant shit talking filters through my head as my body slowly relaxes, and I become in tune with every beat of my heart.

"Thirty seconds," Sergei says through the phone.

I go through the motions, triple checking my calculations based on the conditions; wind speed and direction, alleviation, humidity, and spin drift.

"Twenty."

I wince when Mathijs's body folds from Goldchild's strike.

"Fifteen."

The kingpin stays in his spot, laughing and waving his arm about.

"Ten."

Inhale.

"Five."

Exhale.

"Four."

One heartbeat.

Two.

I pull the trigger.

Three.

The boom echoes through the mountains followed by a cacophony of screams and gunfire. Goldchild drops from the impact.

I don't check if he stays down. I go from man to man, gunning them down so they can't make it any closer to Mathijs. I'm too far away to confirm whether I've successfully killed them. As long as they're too disabled to do more, Sergei and his men can clean the place.

The shouts continue for what must be minutes. My position is compromised, but I can't risk moving and leaving Mathijs open without cover.

Just as I think it, nearby commotion pulls me from the sniper. My hand shoots out for the handgun strapped in the holster at my side. Aiden hisses as he tries to fight off two guys from his position on the ground. With one swift curve of my arm, I fire off two shots, hitting the taller one in the throat, and the other chest. Aiden snaps his attention up to me, jaw dropped.

I revert my attention back to the sniper and continue releasing bullet after bullet. I only stop to replace the magazine, then keep going again until Sergei's voice reaches me.

"The north side is clear."

"The house?" I ask.

"Civilians and hostages only. What's *Edelhert's* status?"

I sweep the area surrounding Mathijs, noting each body littering the ground while Josh unties him from the pole.

"Clear," I answer.

"Good. Stay on watch up there until we roll out."

"Roger."

The line dies, and I let myself close my eyes for just a moment. Relief floods through me, and I let out a breath.

Thank you, TJ. I owe you a drink the next time I see you.

I continue patrolling the compound from a distance, prattling off directions into the receiver to the men on the ground so they can deal with anyone who's still alive. I pause when my phone vibrates with an incoming call from Josh.

Frowning, I search the grounds to find him at the back of the house kneeling next to the second person I shot at tonight, fingers pressed against the man's pulse point.

I answer the call. "What's wrong?"

Josh turns his head to say something to the person behind

him, but no sound comes through the phone. I follow his line of sight to Mathijs, who's standing over Goldchild's body wearing Josh's coat. Despite the distance, he's staring straight at me. There's a pride-filled glint in his eyes that makes me falter.

"What's the distance?"

Warmth unfurls through my body at the sound of Mathijs voice. The corners of my lips tip up and I throw a quick glance at my ring before double checking the computer. Clearing my throat, I say, "One thousand five hundred and two meters."

He smirks. "Zalak Bhatia. Ex-Sergeant of the 75th Ranger Regiment. Eleven Bravo. Special Operations Forces. Codename: *Scorpion.* Two confirmed kills at fifteen hundred meters."

A smile cracks across my face, and I have to chew on the inside of my cheek to try to contain it.

Look at me, Mom. Your beloved daughter just made history.

"Get in the car, Mathijs Halenbeek." I can't help myself from grinning. I got engaged, broke my personal record, killed Goldchild, and got in a car. All in one night. "Stop being a security nightmare."

His ensuing chuckle makes my cheeks ache. "I take it a mountainside wedding is off the table?"

"I'll kill you myself if you don't get out of my shot."

"I love when you talk dirty to me."

"Get out," I growl as I whip open the door into Mathijs's office.

One of the housekeepers and the on-call doctor both send me puzzled looks. It's unlike me to call out orders like this, but unless everyone except Mathijs leaves this room within the next ten seconds, I'm going to lose my shit. I had to travel separately and stay until Sergei cleared me to leave.

I know he's alive.

I know he's fine.

But I need to see him and touch him to get rid of every single doubt clouding my mind.

"I suggest doing as she says before we have another death on our hands," Mathijs muses from his spot on the couch.

The doctor chuckles, then gives some advice I know he won't follow, and by the time we're finally alone, I think I've lost the ability to breathe. A cacophony of black and blue mars his pale face, ringing around his eyes and along his jaw and cheek. I can barely see the glint in his bright green eyes through the swelling and bloody skin.

"I shouldn't have killed the motherfucker," I say, my voice sounding like it comes somewhere from hell. I stalk forward until I'm staring down at him. Tentatively, I touch his mottled skin. "I should have brought him back here and removed every single bone from his body with him wide awake. Death was a fucking mercy compared to what I would have done to him."

Mathijs wraps his fingers around my arm. Fury ruptures through my veins at the sight of the rope marks around his wrists. He presses his bloody lips against the scar on my forearm before twisting my hand to rub the diamond ring.

225

"They don't deserve a place in the history books beside you, *Lieverd*. But their names will be lost to whispers and hidden in the shadows, forgotten to time. You? No one will ever forget you. I'll make sure of it."

I capture his lips with mine, careful not to hurt him. Heat explodes between us as the kiss deepens to a point that probably hurts him. He needs to know how much I care about him—how much I *love* him despite not saying the words. Actions have always spoken louder, and I know without a shadow of a doubt that he's reading what I'm trying to say.

He pulls me onto his lap, then releases a pained groan that has his entire body seizing. I quickly climb off him and give him a stern glare. "We are *not* having sex when you're in this state, Mathijs Halenbeek."

His lips tug up into a strained grin. "But what a way to go."

EPILOGUE

Mathijs
Two years later

"I suggest you let me go. Not many people can piss my wife off and live to tell the tale. She has a bit of a protective streak."

I stare down the barrel pointed at my forehead, then nod toward the bindings tying my wrists to the disgustingly tacky foldout chair.

Props to him, though. He chose a lovely location with a stunning view of the city.

Zalak's brother must share the sentiment since his latest investment involved building this complex from the ground up. Maybe I'll force the council to refuse to grant him any permits for this building, and I'll buy it right from him as a nice little present for my beautiful wife.

"On a separate note, do you mind loosening the ropes? It's a tad tight and I'm not too fond of the burn."

Plus, Zalak was in a good mood when she left to go ax throwing with Sergei this afternoon. I can't imagine she's all too happy about tonight's unfortunate turn of events.

My head whips to the side when the butt of his gun collides with my cheek. "Shut the fuck up. You killed my father."

Ah. Yes. Goldchild's offspring.

At least I think he's Goldchild's. They both have the same sleepy eyes and bad teeth. I honestly didn't care to ask for specifics on whose DNA he shares. I mean, whoever his father is—*was*—he clearly wasn't meant to belong on Earth.

Really, he might not even be Goldchild's son since he hasn't asked for the operation that I inherited from the dearly departed cunt of a man. Although, I have to thank him. With the higher quality counterfeits that he designed, I'm now richer than I could have ever dreamed.

I spit out the crimson liquid to the side, careful not to get it on my clothes.

He shifts his weight and rolls his shoulders before squaring them. I narrowly stop myself from grimacing when he presses the murder machine against my forehead.

"Have you ever heard of the saying, 'Hell hath no fury like a woman scorned'?" I ask, crossing my legs and leaning back into the fucking uncomfortable chair. "My wife can have a bit of a temper. Unfortunately for you, she also has a phenomenal aim."

"Any last words?"

My lips twist with a frown. "Yes, actually. How about *duck*?"

"What—"

I flinch, curling into myself to escape the rain of shattering glass. Warm liquid splatters across my face and stains my brand-new top that I just got tailored.

Goldchild Jr. drops unceremoniously to the floor of the abandoned office, and I squint out of the now-shattered window to the adjacent building a little under a mile away.

I scramble back but end up tipping over with the chair when four more panes of glass explode.

Someone's in a bad mood.

No amount of wiggling and pulling frees my hands from the ropes. So after a minute, I give up. Which is all in good time, really, since Sergei walks in.

"Lovely to see you, old friend."

He grunts in response. Ever the conversationalist.

The bindings loosen around my wrists, and he helps me to my feet, leaving me to rub the tenderness away.

"Mrs. Halenbeek is waiting downstairs," Sergei says before I get a chance to ask.

Mrs. Halenbeek. The sound of that will never get old.

See? This is what I like about him. He's a true go-getter who takes his initiative.

Note to self: get him and his wife tickets to the Bahamas for their anniversary.

I trot up to the newly installed elevators. The doors open quickly, and I use the mirrors to right my clothing. My lips curl in disgust at the four red droplets on my pristine white button-down.

"Do you mind lending me your knife?" I ask once we reach the bottom and the metal doors reopen.

Sergei hands it over without question, and I stab the elevator control panels a few times, then do the same to the outdoor ones so there's no way anyone can use the lifts from the bottom floor. "That's for being an asshole to my wife," I mutter.

A couple thousand dollars of damage won't do much to a tycoon. But word on the street is that he's stretched himself thin on this build. So what's a couple extra expenses?

Zalak waits in the middle of the half-built foyer, sniper strapped to her back while her arms are crossed above her pregnant belly. She's still in the green dress she wore for our dinner date where we had a *stellar* private dining experience. Which ended with her complaining that the baby was pushing against her bladder and that she wanted a foot massage.

I smile at her, but she doesn't return the sentiment.

A shiver runs down my spine at the death glare she shoots my way. If looks could kill, I would have several bullet holes in my body so I'm forced to die slowly and painfully from blood loss.

Sergei, knowing the lashing I'm about to receive, hightails it out to the waiting convoy. *Traitor.*

"*Lieverd*, fancy seeing you here." I plant a kiss on her cheek that does nothing to quell the darkness inside of her.

"I told you not to get out of the car," she says through gritted teeth.

"Have I told you that you look absolutely *radiant* tonight?"

I sidle up to her side and place my hand on her stomach, hoping our daughter will kick and distract her from the fact that I'm—and I'm using Zalak's words here—*incapable of keeping myself safe.*

"Don't even start this shit with me, Halenbeek. My ankles are swollen, my back hurts, and I really need to pee."

In our relationship, there's no question of *who wears the pants.* No. Ours is a question of who's carrying the bigger gun.

After all, I'm here to look pretty next to my wife.

"And despite those things—mistake me if I'm wrong—you still shot at your brother's building five times." I wrap my arm around her waist and direct her to the exit.

"My finger slipped." Then she tacks on, "Nine times."

There are many benefits to having your wife as your unemployed-employed self-appointed bodyguard. The main one being that no matter what happens, or how far I go, she'll kill anyone who attempts to harm me.

And what is that if it isn't true love?

The End.

Acknowledgements

If you've made it this far, thank you for reading.

If you're actually reading this, then let's jump right into the goss.

How did I come up with this book, you ask? Not a clue. We all love a woman in male-dominated industries, so I figured why not get our girl absolutely killing it and doing better than most men in a workplace that breeds misogyny?

Since I wanted her to be badass, there was only one logical answer.

Thus, a star was born—not the twinkling kind, but the supergiants that are days away from becoming a black hole (yes, I studied space in high school and university).

As for Mathijs... I was just challenging myself to write about a blond love interest. The fact that he's like a golden retriever was just a happy coincidence.

Anywho, onto the people who deserve bucket loads of love for making Scorpion a possibility.

Amanda, thanks for getting me drunk and gaslighting me into finishing the book. I wouldn't have survived without you.

Tyla, you kept me sane and gave this book the enthusiasm it should receive.

Kiza, my guy, I owe you one. You are the sole reason my imposter syndrome took a nap for long enough to get this book out on the shelves.

Eve, as always, I love you to the moon and back. You deserve the world and then some for all of your unwavering support and constant cheerleading. You're the best <3

Lisa, you really just pop out banger after banger. Your advice has been superb.

Sebastian, you're a real one for letting me pick your brains since Google has been less than helpful in giving me the answers I need.

Dana LeeAnn, you trooper. We were in the trenches together, and there's no denying that trauma bonding is a real thing. Thank you for all your genius ideas and for being a sounding board for literally everything under the sun.

About the author

From an early age, romance author Avina St. Graves spent her days imagining fantasy worlds and dreamy fictional men, which spurred on from her introverted tendencies. In all her day dreaming, there seemed to be a reoccurring theme of morally grey female characters, love interests that belong in prison, and unnecessary trauma and bloodshed.

Much to everyone's misfortune, she now spends her days in a white collar job praying to every god known to man that she might be able to write full time and give the world more red flags to froth over.

(Update: she's now writing full time)

Also by

Death's Obsession

He's the Grim Reaper, and she's the girl he won't let die.

Skin of a Sinner

You're childhood best friend goes missing for three years, and comes back in the middle of the night to murder your foster family.

Fiery Little Thing

Enemies to lovers, but she's a kleptomaniac, and he's the pyromaniac who burned her house down.

Made in the USA
Columbia, SC
16 September 2024